DETROIT PUBLIC LIBRARY
P9-DDC-152

A King Production presents...

DRAKE II

A NOVEL

JOY DEJA KING
AND CHRIS BOOKER

CHASE BRANCH LIBRARY
17731 W. SEVEN MILE RD.
DETROIT, MI 48235

FEB - - 2018

CH

This novel is a work of fiction. Any references to real people, events, establishments, or locales are intended only to give the fiction a sense of reality and authenticity. Other names, characters, and incidents occurring in the work are either the product of the author's imagination or are used fictitiously, as those fictionalized events and incidents that involve real persons. Any character that happens to share the name of a person who is an acquaintance of the author, past or present, is purely coincidental and is in no way intended to be an actual account involving that person.

ISBN 13: 978-0991389049
ISBN 10: 0991389042
Cover concept by Joy Deja King
Cover Model: Joy Deja King

Library of Congress Cataloging-in-Publication Data;
A King Production
Drake by: Joy Deja King and Chris Booker
For complete Library of Congress Copyright info visit;
www.joydejaking.com

A King Production
P.O. Box 912, Collierville, TN 38027
A King Production and the above portrayal log are trademarks of A King Production LLC

Copyright © 2014 by A King Production LLC. All rights reserved. No part of this book may be reproduced in any form without the permission from the publisher, except by reviewer who may quote brief passage to be printed in a newspaper or magazine.

This Book is Dedicated To My:

Family, Readers and Supporters.
I LOVE you guys so much. Please believe that!!

“I don’t care if we on the run.
Baby as long I’m next to you.
And if loving you is a crime.
Tell me why do I bring out
the best in you.”

— Part II (On The Run)

Chapter 1

Veronica's body lay stiff on the floor of her apartment, and the flashing lights of the forensic unit taking pictures lit up the room. She had to have been lying there for a couple of days due to the odor coming from her decaying body that was still bound by her hands and feet. Duct tape covered her mouth, and her eyes were still open, as though she died of shock.

One of the detectives turned her body over to find that she'd been shot twice in the back of her head, but strangulation marks around her neck determined that the gunshots weren't the cause of death, but rather insurance that she was dead.

Detective Green could smell the rotting body as soon as he entered the apartment complex. When he walked into Veronica's apartment, he was careful not to accidentally step on or touch the evidence that was being processed by other detectives. Being assigned to this case, he was now the lead investigator, and everyone had to answer to him. He wasn't good at too much of anything, but when it came to solving a murder, he was the best in his division. He particularly hated murders that had anything to do with women and children. In fact, Green requested from his supervisors that he be placed on those types of cases alone. "Cause of death?" he asked as he took a piece of chewing gum out of his pocket and placed it in his mouth, not really too bothered by the smell of the dead body.

Detective Mack, who was looking down at Veronica's lifeless body trying his best to collect any evidence, raised his head and said, "The cause of death, I believe, is strangulation. I'd say she's been dead for a couple days now. And from the looks of the place, there had to have been a struggle."

"What about the blood coming from the back of her head?" Green asked, curious as to the amount underneath her.

"Well, the perp shot her after he strangled her just to make sure that the job was done."

Detective Mack went on to explain to Green his theory in detail, having seen this happen one too many times. Every door that he knocked on, either no one answered, or no one had seen or heard anything. The building's superintendent was the one who called the cops after a few of the neighbors complained about a foul odor in the building.

Veronica's jewelry was still in her jewelry box in her bedroom, and over 100-K in cash was left in a dresser drawer. All of the expensive items were still in the apartment, and it didn't look like anything was taken, just broken up.

Green immediately ruled out robbery and quickly determined that this murder was on a more personal level than anything. All he had to do was find out who hated the victim so much they would kill her in such a brutal manner. But the clock was ticking, and with every minute that went by the chances of finding the killer became less likely.

At any rate, someone had to answer for Veronica's death, because Detective Green wasn't going to let up until that happened. *Nobody deserves to die the way Veronica did,* he thought to himself as he stood over her body.

"Wait. There's something in her mouth," Mack said as he peeled the duct tape from her lips. He then pulled out a Timex watch without the band.

"What the hell is a watch doing in her mouth?" Green asked, wondering if this was some type of calling card from the killer. "What time does it say?"

"The time stopped at 1:30 a.m.," Mack said as he passed the watch to Green. "That's probably the time she was killed."

"Or it's just a way to say that her time was up," Green said as he placed the watch into a plastic evidence bag. "Normally, gangs and psychos do shit like this." Green had seen it all before. He used to work in Chicago when he was just a rookie cop about fifteen years ago, and when it came to murder, there weren't many ways a man could die that he hadn't seen or witnessed.

The first thing that he was going to do was go back into her history and find out who this woman was. The person who killed her had to be someone she had dealings with before, or maybe even knew on a more personal level. Nothing and nobody was being ruled out right now.

Green walked into her bedroom and took a good look around. There wasn't any sign of a struggle in the room, but the cell phone sitting on her nightstand caught his attention almost immediately. He grabbed it and took a look through her incoming and outgoing calls, which seemed to be a lot in the few days before she was killed. This was the piece of evidence that he was looking for, and now anyone who had ever called that phone would be questioned about their relationship with Veronica.

Chapter 2

Drake stood in front of Kim and baby Derrick's gravesite at Tucson Cemetery in Bucks County, Pennsylvania. Kim's mother had arranged for the two to be buried together.

Rain clouds in the sky started to form, and a light drizzle began to fall over the tombstones. For some odd reason, it seemed like every time Drake went to visit his family, it would be raining either before or after he got there, making the experience even more dreadful.

With his cane in one hand, he knelt down in front of the gravesite for about an hour, thinking about Kim and the baby and how much he missed them both. It was hard in the beginning, trying to live his life without his family, and often there were times when he thought about committing suicide, thinking that he would be with them.

For the past six months he had been visiting the gravesite once or twice a month, leaving flowers for Kim and a new toy for the baby. It had been about seven months since the shooting, and although he started moving on with his life, he still missed and loved Kim deeply.

Drake's physical health seemed to be making much more progress than his mental. He'd been going to therapy three times a week at the recovery center, along with his own little workouts he did when he was home. The medical bills were sky high for his many surgeries, and seeng as though he didn't have any medical insurance, everything, right down to the medications, was being paid out of pocket. His money was getting low, but he definitely wasn't broke and probably wasn't going to be broke anytime soon. The sound of a car pulling up in the distance snapped Drake out of his thoughts and got his attention. He turned to see who it was and it was exactly who he expected it to be.

Cindy jumped out of a big boy, all white, chrome trimmed Escalade truck, wearing a cropped buttercream leather jacket and pair of tight jeans with knee-high stiletto boots that matched the color of her jacket. Her hair was pulled back in a ponytail, and her diamond hoop earrings brought out the diamond necklace around her neck.

When Cindy walked up, before saying anything to Drake, she paid her respects to Kim and the baby by making the sign of the cross over her chest. She knelt right next to him and grabbed his free hand slowly.

The bond that Drake and Cindy had developed over the past few months was growing even stronger.

Even though they had yet to call what they shared a relationship, they continued to comfort each other during their times of need. There had been a couple of times when they comforted each other a little too much and almost ended up having sex, but the fear of falling in love and the possibility of experiencing losing one another always seemed to ice the heated moments. They never went through with having sex, but they cuddled instead, thinking that was better. But it only brought them closer together on another level, and they had become more emotionally attached to one another.

Cindy respected and understood the love that Drake had for Kim and his son, so she never tried to cross the boundaries of that love. She too still had love for Rodney, her son's father, who had died a few years ago. She always felt like she would be cheating on him if she met someone else, since she and Rodney were happily together when he was murdered.

In a lot of ways Drake felt the same way. He hadn't had sex with anyone since Kim died. He felt like she would be watching him from Heaven. That's probably why he allowed Cindy to come visit the gravesite with him. He wanted Kim to know that Cindy could possibly be the next woman he allowed to be in his life. He wasn't looking for approval, but rather understanding from Kim that it was time for him to start something new.

"I have to go out of town," Cindy said, breaking the silence. "I'll only be gone a couple of days."

"Where are you going?" Drake asked, kissing the headstones of Kim and the baby to say his good-byes for the day.

"I've got to go to Miami to pick something up. My flight leaves in a couple of hours, and I'll be back on Saturday."

"Do you need me to come with you?" he questioned, grabbing hold of her hand as they walked back towards their cars.

"No. I should be alright. Besides, tomorrow is your last day at the recovery center. You've got a lot of people who want to see you."

During the time at the recovery center, Drake inspired a lot of other patients in their recovery process. He worked hard every time he showed up; from the time he signed in until he walked out the door.

What the people didn't know was that he only worked so hard because he wanted to recover from his wounds before Tazz recovered from his, and before Villain got out of jail. That was a never-ending beef, and the only one that was going to survive it, was the one who was the smartest and the strongest.

Cindy got into her truck, but Drake wasn't through talking just yet. He stood at the driver's side door and motioned for her to roll down her window. She had a feeling that it wouldn't be that easy getting out of the city without getting an earful from her now best friend, Drake.

"What are you going to Miami for, Cindy?" he asked as he rested his arms on the door as if he wasn't going to move without getting an answer. He already knew that her drug connect delivered to the front door and it wasn't but four days ago that the last delivery came in, so, she couldn't be going down there for drugs. The dirty money being laundered was based in New Jersey, and that system was set up to perfection, so it couldn't be for that reason. Plus, it was the beginning of winter so a vacation was out of the question. Whatever the reason was, he was concerned and wanted to know. "Now, before you say anything, I want you to remember that since we've known each other, not once did we ever lie to one another, so don't start now," he said, looking her directly in her eyes.

His stare reached down to the depths of her soul. She wanted to tell him the reason for her trip, but if she did it would ruin everything. On the other hand, she just couldn't bring herself to tell him a lie. The only thing that saved her from telling him anything was the loud interruption of her cell phone going off, breaking the awkward silence. She looked down at the phone and saw that it was a call coming in from Miami. "If I tell you why I'm going to Miami, it will ruin the trip for me. You just have to trust me when I tell you that I'm not going down there to do anything stupid. I have some very important things I need to take care of that are personal to me. After me telling you this if you still want to know, then I'll tell you. But if you trust me, let me go without you having to know why. I promise I'll tell you eventually," she stated, staring directly back into Drake's eyes.

Her phone was still ringing, and even though it bothered him like hell not to know, he could only respect her wishes. He had to trust her and everything she had said. She could have easily lied to him and told him anything, but she didn't, and that counted for a lot. He leaned up off of the truck, satisfied at being left in the dark for now, but hoping to eventually know the truth.

Cindy finally answered her phone. "Hello… Yeah, let me call you back in five minutes," she told the person on the other end, then hung up. She turned her attention back to Drake and said, "I need you to stay at my house until I get back. My sister is watching the baby and I hate them being there alone. You think you can do that for me… please?" she begged playfully.

Staying over at Cindy's house wasn't anything new for him. He would spend the night from time to time if he didn't feel like driving home or whenever he didn't feel like sleeping alone. Plus, he and Lil' Rodney got along well, so that wouldn't be a problem.

"Damn, nigga! Who da fuck is dat?" Rick asked, jumping down off of the porch after seeing Amber and Nickie walking on the other side of the street, heading towards the Chinese store about a half a block away.

The county jail had released Rick early from his 11½ to 23 month's sentence. He had pled guilty to a high-speed chase. He only sat for seven months and two days, but if you left it up to him, he might have had you thinking that he just came home from the state penitentiary. He was still hustling on 23rd Street, but he was now under the supervision of Hassan, Cindy's cousin.

Cindy couldn't really trust Rick to run his own neighborhood because of the many problems that he had, like spending all of his money as quickly as he made it. He never admitted to it, but he was also snorting coke.

Rick ran into the Chinese store to holla at Amber, who was ordering a Pepsi and two Dutch Masters by the time he had come in. He could see the Dutches and figured that this was the best time to mention that his block also sold weed.

Amber was sexy as hell to Rick. She was about five feet six inches, and weighed about 140lbs. She was well proportioned with just enough breasts and ass to fill out fitted jeans and a tight t-shirt. A pretty face and lips that always looked wet were enough to make her a must have in Rick's mind.

He had seen her a few times before in the 'hood during the summer, but he never really got the chance to holla at her because he was always working. "You're wifey material, you know that?" he rhetorically asked her flat out.

Amber smiled from ear to ear, flattered by the comment.

Her girlfriend, Nickie, cut in before he could say anything else, jealous that she didn't get the comment first. She wasn't as good looking as Amber was, but she was far from ugly. But it was Amber who got chosen today. "So what? I'm not wifey material?" she snapped back like a usual 'hood rat would do.

"Nah, but you baby momma material! It's almost the same thing. I just happened to see ya girlfriend first," Rick shot back at Nickie so she wouldn't feel no type of way.

He turned back to Amber, who was getting her change from the Chinese lady behind the window. He was so focused on trying to get her phone number that he didn't notice the car that pulled up in front of the store or the two men wearing hoodies that got out of it and headed for the store door. Nickie froze at the sight of the two men coming through the door with guns drawn, and by the time Rick turned around, it was too late.

"You Rick?" one of the gunmen asked, raising the gun up to Rick's head. Rick didn't even get a chance to answer the question before the gunman pulled the trigger, shooting him in the middle of his forehead.

Blood spattered all over Amber's face. She couldn't even bring herself to scream as she watched Rick's body fall to the ground. She just stood there motionless as the shooter stood over Rick and fired three more shots into his face.

Nickie had no problem screaming. She was scared to death, and for a minute she thought that they were going to shoot her too. "Please don't shoot me! Please don't shoot me!" she cried out, hoping that the men got who they came for.

She could have saved her pleas, because the gunmen weren't paying her or Amber any mind. They didn't care whether or not the girls or the Chinese lady got a good look at them. They walked out of the store and got back into the car just as calmly as they did before they entered. Then they pulled off as if they were in no rush.

"I think we got something!" Federal Agent Pesco told Agent Lavinski, slapping the headphones on his ears. "She's calling back the guy from Miami."

The Feds had been watching Cindy for a while now, and not long ago they got permission from the prosecutor to tap her cell phone, house phone and the local phone booth two blocks away from where she lived. They put a tracking device on her truck and car, and had almost 24-hour surveillance of her home. They had two informants who constantly bought small amounts of cocaine from one of her top workers, but neither of the informants had yet to buy the coke directly from Cindy. The Feds knew that she supplied 90% of the city with grade-A cocaine, but they just didn't know where she kept it or where she was getting it. They were hoping that would soon change.

"My flight leaves in about two hours. Is everything good on your end?" Cindy asked Mario, her friend in Miami.

"Yeah, everything is good. Are you going to bring the money with you?" he asked, wanting to make sure that the financial portion of the deal was still agreed upon.

"One-point five million is a lot of money to be getting on an airplane with," she said jokingly. "Don't worry about the money. It's already there," Cindy told him, and then hung up the phone in his ear.

Agent Pesco smiled, thinking that this was it. He was about to catch Cindy red-handed purchasing and transporting cocaine from Florida. Before anything could be done, the evidence the agents had on Cindy—including the new phone conversation she just had with the guy in Florida—had to be taken to the head of the FBI in order to get approval to follow her down to Florida. One-point five million dollars in cocaine was more than enough to put her and her whole operation away for a long time. With any luck, the agents were also hoping that they could get her supplier at the same time. With the evidence they had, it would be more than enough to get the necessary approval but they had to move fast. Her flight left in two hours.

Hassan pulled up and parked a couple of blocks away from the Chinese store that Rick had gotten shot in. He could see the crowd of people covering the sidewalk, and the yellow police tape wrapped around the perimeter of the store. He noticed one of his workers in the midst of the crowd holding on to a young woman who was crying her heart out. As he got closer, he could hear screams and a crying voice that sounded familiar to him. It was Rick's mom.

"They killed my son! They killed my son!" she cried out as she noticed Hassan making his way through the crowd to get to her. "They shot my baby, Hassan!" she continued to scream.

Hassan was well known in the neighborhood by everyone, and Ms. Pepper had been around long enough to watch him grow up. Anything she ever needed, she could call on Hassan, and he would be there. She was like an aunt to him, and seeing as though Ms. Pepper and Ms. Matty, Hassan's mom, were best friends, he used to call her "Auntie" when he was younger. This was all before she even had Rick. *Who da fuck would want to kill Rick?* Hassan thought to himself as he held onto Ms. Pepper while she went hysterical.

He looked across the street and could see Amber and Nickie sitting in the back of an unmarked car with the door open. A detective was questioning both of them about what had happened. Hassan knew who Nickie was, but he didn't know Amber, who had blood spatter on her shirt. He acted on instinct, letting go of Ms. Pepper and walking across the street to where the girls were. He made it past three police officers before being stopped by a fourth, about ten feet away from the unmarked car. "Who shot 'em, Nickie?" Hassan yelled over the officer's shoulder who was holding him back.

"Who did it?" he yelled out again before being pulled away by another cop who knew him from the neighborhood.

All of the crying that Ms. Pepper was doing had Hassan in his feelings, which made him step out of character. He knew that Nickie knew who had shot Rick. She was a true 'hood rat, and there weren't too many people in South Philly that she didn't know. Hell, she knew a lot of people in other neighborhoods also. Ninety-percent of gossip came from 'hood chicks. They knew everything about everybody, and if they didn't know, they would find out sooner or later. They were the best people to go to if you needed any information. 'Hood chicks have their own method and system for getting information, and most of the time it was accurate.

The sight of detectives and police officers surrounding the girls forced Hassan to retreat back into the crowd before he got one last look at Amber. Even if she didn't know who it was that shot Rick, he still had a few questions of his own for her. As for right now, the police and the detectives made their way into the crowd, questioning any and everyone they came in contact with.

Hassan quickly came to his senses and realized that he had drugs in his car. That was enough for him, and he got the hell out of there fast, but not before telling Ms. Pepper that he would find the person who killed her son. That he promised, and Hassan never broke a promise.

Chapter 3

Villain walked into the visiting room with a blue jumpsuit on. Seeing as no one had come to see him in the past few months, he was looking forward to seeing a familiar face. He'd been in the Virginia County Jail for the past five months, awaiting a bail hearing for the gun charge. The judge scheduled a bail hearing for next week, and even if he did make bail in Virginia, he would be taken back to Philly to face attempted murder charges on Peaches.

"What's good wit' you, playboy?" Tazz asked as he stood up to embrace his friend. "Before you say anything, I know it's been a while, but I've been on the streets taking care of some things."

"Nah, bro, everything's good. I'm just happy to see you. I've been trying to call the house, but nobody answers the phone around there," Villain joked. "So, what's been going on?"

"Aw, bro, you're not going to believe this, but I'm back in the streets."

"What do you mean, you're back in the streets? What about the nightclubs and the real estate?" Villain asked, shocked at what he just heard Tazz say.

"That type of spotlight from the club had me too hot in the streets. As long as I'm getting money, I'll always be a target, and the life I used to live made it easier for folks to get to me. Don't get me wrong, I still rent out houses to Section 8, but the nightclub thing is over. I'm back in the 'hood where I belong."

What Tazz was saying didn't make too much sense to Villain. It was either Tazz wasn't telling him everything, or he was just going crazy. He had the perfect setup. He sold drugs, had property, and owned two nightclubs, which most of his drug money was laundered through. Villain could understand the part about being an easy target in the spotlight, but that's the reason Tazz hired so much security. Besides, robberies come with the game.

The one thing Villain was right about was the fact that Tazz wasn't telling him everything. The truth of the matter was that Tazz was broke. Besides the two nightclubs and the few houses he owned in the city, he really didn't have too much of anything. Drake had taken it all, and what money he did have left over went to things like Villain's lawyer fees, property taxes, day-to-day living, and most costly, medical bills. Tazz took a tough blow that gave him no other choice, but to go back to where it all started... hustling from the bottom and working his way up.

"How's Christina doing?" Villain asked.

"She's maintaining. She somewhat stressed and scared thinking Drake somewhere plotting revenge against me, which means she might be in danger. So I moved her out of the state until shit dies down. She wants us to move to Kentucky permanently by next year."

"Kentucky?" Villain asked, wondering why there of all places. "What the hell is out in Kentucky?"

"Nothing at all," Tazz answered with a smile.

"What about Drake? What's the last thing you heard on him?" Villain asked on a more serious note.

Tazz hadn't heard too much of anything about Drake. The last time he saw him was at Villain's hearing. He knew that he wasn't that far away as long as Villain had the opportunity to come home soon; that is if Peaches turned up dead or just didn't show up to court for trial, or whatever the case might be. Tazz wanted his revenge just as badly as Drake wanted his, so until Tazz got what he wanted, he was going to sit back and wait for Drake to lift his head up from whatever hole he was hiding in.

Tazz looked Villain in the eyes and said, "I won't rest well at night until dat nigga is placed in the grave right next to his girl and his little boy. Damn, bro! I got to get you home!"

"Well, you know I got a bail hearing next week, and the lawyer said that my bail will be around 10-K. But I still got the Philadelphia detainer for that shit wit' Peaches. My bail for the Philly case was set at 750-K, but the 10% dropped it down to 75-K," Villain explained, a little excited about the possibility of getting released.

"Damn! You know I got you on the first bail, but my money is kinda tied up right now. I'm trying to make a move wit' a new connect." Instead of just telling Villain the truth about being broke, Tazz let his pride get in the way and sold his friend a dream. He did have a meeting with a possible new supplier, but he was trying to get something on credit; something he would most likely have a problem doing seeing as he had been out of the loop for the past six months.

Another problem Tazz had to face even if he did get credit for a large amount of coke, was that 95% of the clientele he once had now belonged to Cindy and her crew. The coke she'd been getting was grade-A, and cheap. Stepping into the ring with her at this point would be frivolous. He wouldn't be able to sell an ounce in the city, let alone pump large amounts of weight. If Cindy ever got wind of someone else selling big weight, she would definitely send her little goon squad so you would get an understanding about who's running the city. She laid the blueprint down, and all anyone else could do was ride with her or get rolled over, and that included Tazz.

The Feds had been following Cindy for the past 24 hours, and they still hadn't seen her do anything suspicious. She flew from Philly to Miami, got right into a rental car, then went straight to her Hotel and checked in. She'd been there ever since, and no one came or left her room all day. This was starting to frustrate Agent Pesco, but he knew that he had to be patient in order to get what he was looking for.

"She didn't come all this way just to sit in a hotel," Pesco said to Lavinski as they sat in a hotel room down the hall from Cindy.

"She's going to move. Just give her some time. Trust me—"

Lavinski couldn't even finish his sentence before the call came over his radio informing him that Cindy was on the move. Two federal agents from Miami were assisting in the case. Agent Scrubs and Agent Heart had set up surveillance outside of the hotel, and had a clear view down the second floor hallway where Cindy and the other two agents' rooms were.

As she moved, Pesco and Lavinski did too, and followed her outside. She jumped into her car and pulled off with Heart and Scrubs tailing her from a safe distance. It didn't take but a few minutes for Lavinski and Pesco to catch up, also keeping a safe distance.

It was 2:30 in the afternoon, and Cindy was heading down Biscayne Boulevard when her cell phone rang. She looked down and saw that it was Hassan. She was unaware of the news that she was about to hear. "Yo, what's good, cousin?" she answered in a chipper voice.

"Rick got shot."

Cindy almost swerved off of the road when she heard that. Even though she and Rick weren't vibing with each other right now, she still had love for him like a little brother. Hell, she practically raised him since he was 13 years old; that is, as far as the streets go. "Is he alright?" she asked frantically, hoping that it wasn't that serious.

"They shot him in his head, cousin. He died instantly," Hassan told her, getting upset at the thought of Ms. Pepper crying on his shoulder. It was too much. Cindy had to pull over before she got into an accident.

This move confused the Feds who were following her because she suddenly pulled over to the side of the road, forcing them to drive past her and possibly losing her, or to pull over also and possibly drawing attention to themselves. Agent Pesco pulled over first, seeing as he was further behind her than Agent Scrubs.

Cindy couldn't bring herself to cry. It wasn't that she didn't care, but more so that she never really cried over anyone except when her dad died, and when her son's father was killed. Other than that, she was strong when it came to dealing with death. Her grieving process was quick, only lasting a couple of hours, if that. "I'll get back into the city tonight," she said, hanging up the phone and pulling back out into the road.

There were a couple of more lights before she pulled into an exotic luxury car dealership. They had almost every kind of car you could think of, from Rolls Royces, Ferraris, Porsches, Bentleys, Aston Martins, Bugattis, BMWs and Lamborghinis. This place had it all.

Agent Pesco and Agent Scrubs pulled into a Dodge dealership directly across the street. They just knew that Cindy wasn't there to buy a car.

"And what better place to sell cocaine in than this!" Agent Lavinski told his partner as they watched Cindy get out of her rental car and make her way inside the dealership.

"If she comes out with a bag, we'll wait until she gets off of the premises before we arrest her. We don't want to give the people inside a heads up that we're on to them," Agent Pesco communicated over the radio to Scrubs and Heart.

When Cindy did exit the dealership an hour later she didn't have a bag with her, and she got right back into the rental car and pulled off.

Pesco directed Scrubs to follow her, while he went to have a look around the dealership and possibly ask a few questions while he was there. He couldn't figure out why Cindy went to a dealership, of all places.

On her way back to the airport, Cindy's phone started to ring again. This time it was Joshua, one of the workers at the car dealership she had just left. She quickly answered, hoping that nothing was wrong concerning their deal. "Hello."

"Ah, Cindy, I thought you should know that no more than a couple of minutes after you left, the Feds came in and asked a few questions about why you were here. I told them you were interested in buying a car."

Suddenly, Cindy had a feeling that someone was following her. She looked into her rearview mirror to see if she noticed any of the cars behind her, but she didn't. Then everything came rushing to her brain at once. She thought about Rick getting killed, the Feds watching her and possibly having enough information to indict her, little Rodney having to grow up without his mother or father, and oddly, she thought about Drake and how much he reminded her of Rodney. Cindy wasn't ready for her life to be over because for her, a new chapter was just beginning.

Tazz walked into the pet store on Cityline Avenue where he was supposed to meet the new connect. He wasn't sure what to expect. The store smelled like shit and piss. An old friend of Tazz's set the meeting up for him but made no promises that he would get what he was looking for. Make no mistake, Tazz knew how to hustle from the muscle, and if given the opportunity with the right amount of cocaine, he could become a problem in the city and a major threat to Cindy and her organization.

"Interested in buying a dog?" a short, Mexican looking man asked, coming from the back of the store.

"No, I'm good," Tazz answered, blowing the floor worker off with an attitude. Little did he know, he was blowing off Hector, his possible new connect.

Hector sure had a way of disguising himself to look like an average, everyday nine to five worker. Being the biggest drug supplier on the East Coast, this took a lot of attention off of him. He also had a thing about wanting to be the "Average Joe" person who works hard for a living as opposed to making fast money the easy way by selling drugs. Life can get boring when you're the boss, everything changes, and the fun of hustling your way to the top is over once you get there. That's the reason why he didn't mind getting paid minimum wage, and getting his hands dirty in the process. But right now, it was time for him to clock in on his other job. "Are you interested in buying something else? Maybe the very thing you came here for in the first place," he said, grabbing a bag of birdfeed off of a shelf next to Tazz.

Tazz didn't catch on immediately, but then he quickly realized that this was his man. "Hector?" he asked to be sure that he was talking to the right person.

"Yeah, talk to me," Hector acknowledged while grabbing handfuls of birdfeed and putting it into the cages.

"Look. I'm trying to buy a few bricks, and I was hoping that you could front me something on top of it."

"I don't do fronts. And if all you want are a few bricks, you're in the wrong place. I don't answer the phone for anything less than 100 bricks. I thought that Barbosa told you that when he set this meeting up."

"Yeah, he did, but he also knows that I'm good for it. I was robbed and shot a few months back and they took everything."

Hector cut him off before he could go on with his sad story. This wasn't the way he did business, and Tazz was starting to get on his nerves. "I don't have anything to do wit' your situation. I'm a businessman, Tazz, not a loan shark. You wanna buy some cocaine from me, then buy some cocaine. If you're looking for charity, there's a Salvation Army two blocks down the street," he said, becoming irritated.

The way Hector was talking to Tazz was disrespectful, and he felt every bit of it, including a little humiliation to top things off. Ending the meeting, Hector began to walk off to get back to his temporary job in the pet store.

Tazz had to think fast and make an offer that Hector couldn't refuse. "I have two nightclubs. I'll sell them to you for a good price," he said, getting Hector's attention. "The buildings are paid for, and the taxes are reasonable."

Hector never thought about running that kind of business, mainly because he never considered buying a club before. Obviously he had the money to do so, but it was never on his agenda… that is until today. Club Hector's, he thought to himself. The name was corny, but when you have the money to blow, he could call it whatever he wanted. "How much do you want for your clubs?" he asked while walking back towards Tazz.

Selling drugs wasn't the only thing that Hector was good at, and the start of his own nightclub sounded like fun. Girls, music, and dancing were all the things he was missing in his life. He surely could use the club as a front to launder the amount of money he was making selling drugs, which was in the millions.

Tazz wasn't thrilled about the decision he was making, but it was his only way to get back on top. Any real hustler could tell you that it's not about the setback; it's about the get-back.

The flight back to Philly wasn't that bad. Cindy was tired though, wanting nothing more than a hot shower and something to eat.

She walked into the house and spotted Ebony on the couch asleep with the TV on. Rodney must be in his bed, she thought to herself. She looked around the house to see that the baby had had a field day with his toys. The cleaning process would have to wait until the morning, because after the hot shower, it was bedtime.

Cindy went upstairs to her bedroom and was surprised to see little Rodney asleep in her bed with Drake. *He must have sneaked into the bed after everyone went to sleep. That's what he always does.* She took a good look at how handsome they both looked lying there in dreamland. She took Rodney to his room and got right into the shower.

The hot water beading over her body was exactly what she needed. The thoughts of Rick and the Feds watching her washed down the drain with the rest of the water.

With a large towel wrapped around her body, she walked into the bedroom to find that Drake was still asleep, lying flat on his stomach. His still body looked so inviting and this tingling sensation shot through her pussy at the sight of him lying in her bed. The more she stared at him, the wetter she became. It had been a few years since she had the pleasures of a man in her life. It was as though she couldn't control herself any longer. She had no desire to settle for a bunch of heavy kisses she normally had with Drake before something stopped them from going the extra mile.

Taking the towel off, she was completely naked. This was as far as she ever went, and at this point, there was no turning back. She climbed into the bed and crawled up under the blanket to meet Drake's half-naked body. He was rocking nothing but a pair of sweatpants. She climbed on top of his back, admiring his ripped upper body. She leaned over and kissed one of his scars from a bullet wound. This woke him up.

"I thought you weren't coming back until tomorrow," he said in a groggy voice with his eyes still shut.

"I missed you," Cindy returned, laying another warm kiss to his other bullet wound scar.

The second kiss woke him up even more, and this time he had to crack his eyes open. He turned over onto his back, only to see Cindy's bare breasts and fully naked body on top of him. He never saw her completely naked, and there she was, sitting on top of him and staring him straight in the eyes. She leaned in to steal another kiss, this time on the lips.

Damn her body so warm, Drake thought to himself as he grabbed the lower part of her back and pressed her stomach up against his. "What are you doing, Cindy?" he managed to get out through the flutter of kisses she was giving him. He was thinking that this was just a phase that she was going through, like the many other times when she kissed him.

Cindy didn't say a word. She sat up, grabbed hold of Drake's boxers and sweatpants, pulled them off and threw them on the floor. She lightly ran her hands across his ripped stomach before kissing every inch of his six-pack. His dick was massive; long, black, thick, and he wasn't even hard yet. She took one look at it and almost had an orgasm just imagining him filling up her insides. She led a trail of warm wet kisses down his stomach.

Drake quickly grabbed her before she could put his dick in her mouth. As much as he wanted to feel the warmth of her mouth around his hardened tool, he had a lot more respect for her than to let her go down on him the first time they had sex.

Unfortunately, Cindy could care less about how he felt. She grabbed both of his wrists and pinned them to the bed. "Let me do me," she said in a seductive tone, giving Drake a gaze that told him not to stop her again.

Warm kisses led a path down his stomach once again. This time she let her tongue do most of the navigating. She kissed the top of his dick, which by now was rock hard. Without using her hands, she licked up and down the shaft, and then kissed the head again. She looked up at Drake to see his reaction when she took his manhood into her mouth and down her throat. She sucked it slowly, letting warm spit run down his balls and onto the bed. Her mouth was so warm and wet that it made a swishing noise every time her head went up and down. She took Drake's hand and placed it on the back of her head, wanting him to guide her mouth. She sped up and sucked his dick faster and faster, and deeper and deeper down her throat.

"Oh shit!" Drake moaned while watching his dick disappear and then reappear with every stroke of her mouth. *I have to warn her,* he thought to himself, feeling the tingling sensation right before he would bust a nut. "Stop! I'm about to cum!" he said as he tried to lift her head up.

Cindy grabbed his hand and pinned it back onto the bed. She sped up again, adding more warm spit into her mouth and thrusting his dick as far down her throat as she could get it. She could feel his body starting to tense up. His legs locked up and he grabbed a handful of the sheets and blanket as if he was holding on for dear life. She could feel his dick pulsating. The cum shot up the shaft of his dick and the warmness filled her mouth.

Drake grabbed Cindy's head and pulled her up. He grabbed her by her waist and rolled her over so that she was lying on her back. Her breasts were firm, and her nipples were hard and sensitive to the touch. He looked her in the eyes, and then leaned in for a kiss, planting his full, thick lips against hers with a slight twist of his tongue, playing tag with hers. He grabbed a handful of her breast with one hand and leaned down to suck on the other one, twirling his tongue around her nipple.

Cindy's pussy was pulsating from his every touch, and was dripping with milky honey and awaiting the arrival of Drake's dick to penetrate deep down inside of her. He attempted to go down on her to return the oral favor, but she stopped him, wanting nothing more than to feel his manhood inside of her. "Just put it in!" she moaned, spreading her legs wider.

With every inch that went inside, Cindy moaned. She lifted her legs higher and relaxed the muscles so that he could push the rest of his meat inside of her. Her pussy was tight and wet, and she wrapped her arms around him to pull his body closer to hers. She couldn't keep her lips off of his. She thrust her tongue into his mouth with uncontrollable moans from every stroke of his dick.

After getting used to the size of his dick, Cindy grabbed onto his ass and directed his strokes to the tempo she wanted, which was slow and deep. The long stroking stopped, and the deep digging began. She arched her back slightly and pressed her pelvis against his, and pushed his meat inside of her until it couldn't go any further. She swayed her hips back and forth as though she wanted him to reach her stomach. Her walls became snug and tight, and the feeling of a huge orgasm was coming on. She held on for dear life as he dug himself deeper and deeper into her, building up his own release point.

"Drake! Drake!" she whispered. "Oh, Drake! I'm cumming! Deeper! Deeper!" she cried out into his ear. It felt so good that she began to literally cry out. She exploded. The orgasm shot through her entire body and during that time Drake also released his thick, warm cream. She felt it all inside of her.

Drake pulled away from Cindy's lips, but still kept his dick inside of her. He looked into her eyes and wiped a tear from the side of her face. "You know this changes everything," he said.

She reached up and grabbed the back of his head and pulled him back down to her lips so that she could kiss him. She couldn't control her giggles as their lips connected. They showered each other with soft, slow pecks.

"What's so funny?" he asked, pulling away from her kisses once again.

"You wanna know what's so funny?" Cindy asked, still smiling from ear to ear.

"Yeah. Tell me," he shot back, and thrust his still rock hard dick into her, which caused her to suck in a deep breath.

"I think I'm in love with you, Drake," she said as another tear rolled down the side of her face.

Chapter 4

About thirty cars lined up back to back for Rick's funeral that took place in South Philly where he was born and raised. Almost everyone from the neighborhood showed up, including Nickie and Amber, who were personally escorted by Hassan. He had a lot he wanted to discuss with the both of them before the day was over, concerning what happened in the Chinese store.

Drake pulled up behind Hassan's car, and for a moment Hassan didn't recognize the 745 BMW, nor who was occupying it. He knew Drake from the 'hood, but never really got a chance to keep up with the different kinds of cars he switched up with. There were a couple of other things he didn't know about Drake, and when Cindy hopped out of the passenger side of his ride, it blew his mind. He looked at Cindy, then back at Drake, who was also getting out of the car.

"Yo-o-o-o! This is a good look!" Hassan said, and covered his mouth with a shocked but happy expression on his face. He, out of everyone, knew exactly what the both of them had been through with their prior relationships, and thought off the bat that this was a perfect match. It didn't get any better than having two of South Philly's most powerful people coming together and dictating the direction the city was now heading in.

"Where's Ms. Pepper?" Cindy asked, wanting to pay her respects to Rick's mother before she did anything else.

"She's up front," Hassan replied, and leaned in to get a hug from his little cousin. "While you're up there, tell her we're ready back here whenever she is."

Cindy hadn't been in the 'hood much lately, mainly because she really didn't have a reason to be in the streets. She had a good setup to the point where she didn't even have to touch any of the drugs she sold. Most of the street business went through Hassan, so most of the time all she had to do was pick up money a few times a week. The money she did make from selling drugs was being laundered through a couple of her legal businesses she started, one of which was a condom business. She invested a few thousand dollars into making her very own condom brand called "Lucky". Although the brand didn't sell that well in stores, she used the small business to write off taxes from her drug money.

By the time the viewing and burial of Rick's body was over, everyone was tired and worn out from crying. Ms. Pepper was having a dinner afterward, so most of the people went with her to the ballroom on Cityline Avenue where it was being held.

Another small group consisting of Cindy, Drake, Hassan, Amber, Nickie, James, Lil' P, and Rick's crazy cousin, Pooh from North Philly, met at the house on 23rd Street to try to find out just what had happened to Rick.

The conversation started with Amber explaining the events that took place on that day. It all happened so fast that she really couldn't remember what the two guys that came into the store looked like. She definitely couldn't see the second gunman because he was standing outside the door where Nickie was heading to before the shots rang out. All she could see from the shooter was that he had a black automatic pistol, and he smelled like Muslim oil.

This could have been anybody. Mostly everyone in Philly wore Muslim oil; even non-Muslims.

"Nickie, what did you see?" Hassan asked, seeing that she was very quiet. *She's got to know something,* he thought to himself, waiting for her to answer the question.

"I think I've seen one of the guys before. The shooter… I think I saw him before on the other side of Broad Street, near Christian Street," Nickie said, unsure, but trying her best to remember where she had seen his face before.

"By Christian Street?" Cindy shot back quickly, now focusing harder on what Nickie was saying. The first thing that came to her mind was the dude, Chris, that she murdered awhile back, and the possibility of retaliation from his people. Christian Street was probably the only street she didn't have control over. After the shooting in the bar, she left that little section of the city alone, afraid that someone would eventually get bold enough to tell the police that she was the one who pulled the trigger. *But who could possibly want to retaliate after all this time?* she asked herself, hoping that this wasn't the case.

"Who da fuck is on Christian Street?" Pooh asked, noticing the change in Cindy's attitude. She didn't want to jump to any conclusions, so Cindy declined to answer his question. But Pooh wasn't satisfied with what was going on, and he had no idea who Cindy was so he started yelling and screaming in her direction. Drake was the first person to stand up in Cindy's defense, beating James, her number one shooter to the punch.

Before Drake could pull his ratchet out, Cindy stopped him, knowing that Pooh didn't have a clue as to what he was about to get himself into. "Babe!" she yelled out to Drake. *Oh my God! I can't believe I just called him Babe in front of everyone!* she thought to herself after she realized what she had just said. "Look. We're not going to scream at each other, because it's not going to help find the nigga who shot Rick. Whoever shot him, did it for a reason, and we've got to try and pull together and find out who did it before the cops do. I want the person who did this to be six-feet under, just like Rick is, and I want him to have a closed casket funeral."

Drake and Hassan were still tripping off the fact that Cindy called Drake "Babe" in public. Hassan didn't know that it was that serious between the two of them, and neither did anyone else in the room for that matter.

"Hassan, I want you to drive Nickie around the way to see if she recognizes anybody," Cindy directed, trying not to be too specific about the location of Chris' boys in the event that Pooh wanted to play Superman. "Pooh, I need you to go with James to take Ms. Pepper this money. Lil' P, open the shop back up for the night shift. And Amber, stay out of trouble!" she ordered everyone before getting up to leave.

Everybody left the house at the same time like a football team coming out of a huddle. James led the way, followed by Pooh, Amber, then Nickie and Cindy. Drake brought up the rear while Lil' P stayed back. Total silence took over while everyone poured out onto the sidewalk.

Nickie turned to look down the block and noticed a guy standing on the corner with a black hoodie on. Drake, who was still at the top of the steps, noticed the same thing, and an additional hooded man walking up from the opposite direction.

"Oh my God! That's him, y'all!" Nickie said in a low voice, not wanting to draw attention to herself.

Drake wasted no time. He pulled his weapon from his waistband and fired the first couple of shots at the hooded gunman walking up from the opposite direction. The guy dipped behind a car, pulled out his weapon and returned fire into the crowd. Cindy, Amber and Nickie immediately dropped to the ground. The gunman who was standing on the corner had quickly armed himself and also took refuge behind a car.

Pooh and James, whose guns were drawn, both fired in the direction of the gunman at the corner, knocking holes the size of golf balls into the car and shattering the windows.

The gunman never got the chance to return fire. Hearing the hail of bullets coming in his direction, he took off running back around the corner he had come from.

Cindy, who was still lying on the ground and angry that she didn't have her gun, got a good look at the gunman before he turned the corner. She recognized his face from somewhere.

All the time, the second gunman continued to fire at the crowd as he backed up. One bullet hit Hassan in his left arm, and another hit Pooh in his stomach, buckling him to his knees but not stopping him from emptying the rest of his clip in the gunman's direction.

Hassan went to fire at him, but the slide snapped back, indicating that he was out of bullets. Drake stepped up, but his gun was empty as well. The gunman saw all of this, and instead of continuing to back up, he started to come towards them, seeing an open opportunity.

Pooh thought fast and reached into his jacket like he had something. He was faking. He didn't have a damn thing, but the gunman wasn't going to take any chances, especially not knowing how many shots he had left. He turned around and ran as fast as he could down the block and disappeared in broad daylight.

Cindy jumped up from the ground to check to see if everyone was all right. Pooh went from his knees to flat out falling on the ground, holding his stomach and squirming from the pain the bullet was causing.

Lil' P ran out of the house, took a good look at Pooh, and then darted for his car that was sitting on the corner, all shot up.

"Hold on, Pooh! We're going to get you to a hospital!" Cindy told him as she knelt down next to him in the street. You could hear police sirens in the distance, and they were quickly getting closer.

Lil' P pulled up and Drake put Pooh in the back seat. Lil' P pulled off before Drake could close the car door. The cops were too close for anyone to get into their cars and leave, so they ran back into the house, closed and locked the door. No more than thirty seconds later the police swarmed the block from both ends. There wasn't a soul outside, and it looked like a ghost town.

"Hassan, are you good?" Cindy asked him. She noticed the blood on his jacket.

"Yeah. I think it went in and out," he said as he took his jacket and shirt off to check.

"Who da hell was that?" Nickie shouted as she frantically looked around the room to see if anyone had any answers. This was the second shooting in a week that she and Amber had been involved in, and she was beginning to think that Rick had nothing to do with these men shooting up the neighborhood.

Everyone in the room was thinking the same thing, and the visions of the shooter's face that Cindy recognized was picking at her brain. She couldn't place a name with the face or the place where she knew him. All she knew right then was that the police were driving up and down the block. As she peeked out of the window, she knew that she would never be able to concentrate with all the police action. It would have to wait, but it will eventually come to her. And when it did, it'll be on and poppin'.

Coming back into the city never felt better, even if it was by way of the county jail's transportation unit. Villain had finally made bail from his case in Virginia, but he still had to deal with the detainer he had in Philadelphia for the attempted murder of Peaches. His bail in Philly was a little high, but payable. And if paid, he would be back on the streets. Until then, he'd be housed at the county jail on State Road in maximum security.

Upon getting to the jail and going through the processing formalities, Villain made his first phone call to none other than Tazz. His heart was racing because the taste of freedom was at his fingertips. Most people in the county jail couldn't make a high bail, so they would have to sit and wait until the bail was lowered or it was time to go to trial. A lot of guys also took a guilty plea, not wanting to take their chances losing at trial and getting more time.

Tazz quickly accepted the call once he heard it was Villain. "What's good, lil' bro?" he answered, happy to hear that Villain was back in the city.

"Aw man, one step closer to freedom," Villain shot back, happy to hear Tazz's voice. "I got a hearing in two days for my detainers. Once they get lifted, I can post bail."

"Yeah, well, I got some important business to deal wit' right now, but as soon as I make this move, the first thing I'ma do is pay ya bail. It's going to take me about a week or so, but I got you."

"Look, Tazz. If you don't have the money right now, don't worry about it. I put some money up for times like this. All I need you to do is go get it. If there's one thing I learned from you, it was to spend and save my money wisely."

"Yeah, I wish I would have listened to my own advice!" Tazz said in a disappointed tone.

"Damn, bro! What's going on?" Villain asked with concern.

"Nothing, bro. It's something we'll talk about when you get home. Right now, just keep ya money. Let me worry about the bail situation."

Villain could sense that something was wrong with Tazz. He was surprised that he didn't already have the bail money ready and on deck. And with that, he thought about the actual loss that Tazz took during the entire ordeal. The amount was in the millions, including his lawyer. He wanted to do something to help, even if it meant giving up his last. Villain would rather sit for another week or so in order to help his friend get back on his feet. He knew that Tazz wouldn't let him sit any longer than necessary. His love and trust for Tazz was beyond any love two brothers with the same blood could have. He had put away 55-K for a rainy day, and it was at Tazz's disposal.

For the past few weeks, at least a few times a day Cindy and Drake had been having some of the most mind-blowing sex nonstop. Cindy definitely seemed to be on a mission to make up for all the years she had went without and today was no different than the others.

After another sex session, the sounds of heavy breathing could be heard in the room, and Drake wrapped his arms around Cindy. Even though she was no longer being penetrated, she continued to shake from the orgasm she had experienced. She snuggled her head into his chest, captivated by the small kisses he placed on her forehead, and the way his hand lightly glided up and down her back. She didn't want to leave this position, feeling a sense of security only a man could give. Since being with Drake, he brought out the softer side of her. She didn't have to be this big time, murdering drug dealer gangsta. She could be a woman… or rather the girly, feminine type.

"You want some water?" Drake asked her, brushing a lock of hair from her face and placing it behind her ear.

She really didn't want him to move, but the dry mouth kicked in from exhaustion and the need for water was necessary. "Only if you promise to hurry back," she answered, and kissed the lower part of his lip.

DRAKE II

While Drake was downstairs, Cindy's phone rang. It wasn't just the average ring though. The sound of Reggaeton music filled the air, which only meant one thing; Hector was calling. She would have ignored it, but it was odd that he would call when she hadn't put in an order for a shipment. The only time he called was if he were telling her what time the delivery would take place. "Hello," she answered, sitting up in bed.

"*Hola,* mama. I'm sorry to bother you, but I need you to call me back in two minutes," Hector said, and then hung up.

This only meant that he wanted to discuss something concerning drugs, and the only way he could do that is if Cindy called from a different, prepaid throwaway phone. She had a few of those lying around, and every time she used it for more than a few days she would trash it and start using a brand new one. She quickly reached in the nightstand drawer next to her bed and grabbed one of the prepaid phones to call Hector back.

"Listen," he answered. "A good friend of mine has a friend that needs to buy a couple of keys. It's hardly enough for me to consider leaving the house for. I was wondering if you wanted the business," he explained.

"Yeah, sure, Hector. Whatever you need," Cindy replied, eagerly wanting to stay on Hector's good side. "Take the number that popped up on your caller ID and have him call me."

"Will do. I also wanted to sit down and have lunch with you one day soon so we could talk about better prices for you. You just give me a call and we'll set something up, okay?"

"Okay, I'll give you a call," she said, excited about the talk of better prices.

Cindy had been doing business with Hector for a while now. Every time she went to buy cocaine from him her money was always straight, and she was never late on a pick up. He respected her for that, especially since it was a woman who did more and better business than most of the men he dealt with.

Drake came back into the room with a pitcher of water and two glasses, all the while wearing his birthday suit. "I leave you for one minute and you're already talking on the phone!" he joked, passing her a glass of water.

He couldn't get another word out before her prepaid phone rang. They both looked at the phone, then at one another. "If you tell me not to answer it, I won't," Cindy said, not wanting to break the mood.

Drake knew that it had something to do with business, and the last thing he wanted her to do was stop being who she was, mainly because that's the person he fell in love with. She was a different breed. She was every thug's dream wife, and more. To make her something other than what she was would be uncivilized.

Agents Pesco, Lavinski, and the prosecutor sat in a room discussing how much evidence they had against Cindy so that they could indict her for racketeering, distribution of cocaine, firearms violations, and other crimes within her organization. Most of the main evidence they had to put her away for life was only circumstantial and wouldn't hold up in the court of law, especially with the kind of lawyer she had.

Joseph Ponts, the United States Prosecutor, was at the head of this case, and his success in obtaining convictions was about 99%. In his eight years of being a prosecutor, he only lost four cases.

"So, what all do we have so far on this girl?" Ponts asked the agents, trying to get a feel of what he was working with.

"Well, we know that Cindy is running a small but strict street level organization based in South Philadelphia. When we first started investigating her, we managed to contract two direct sales. Both purchases were nine ounces of powder cocaine. About two months later, our confidential informant made two more purchases directly from her; the first being one key of cocaine, and the second being eighteen ounces of crack. After that, no other purchases were made directly from her. She has a second-in-command, Tyree Gibson a.k.a. Hassan who does the bulk of the transactions while Cindy stays at home with her son," Pesco stated while passing pictures of Hassan, Drake and Cindy across the table to Ponts.

Pesco continued. "Over the past eight months rival big-time drug dealers in her neighborhood turned up dead, and several gun battles occurred on her main corner on 23rd Street; one as recently as a week ago. Our informant said that Cindy is the biggest thing in Philadelphia right now, and probably the most feared as well."

"Well, I think we have enough on her for drug trafficking. But the amount of drugs you've got on her doesn't carry that much time," Ponts chimed in. "So, if you could get more on her, I can give her a life sentence, or maybe even get her to turn on her supplier. Do you have any idea where she's getting her drugs from?" Ponts asked, leaning back in his chair.

"Our resources are limited. We don't have enough funds to tail her 24/7, but we've got a slight idea of where she's getting them. We did follow her to Florida a couple of weeks ago, but all she did was stay at a hotel most of the time, with the exception of her going to a car dealership. Other than that, nothing," Lavinski said.

"Alright, look. In order for me to go to the magistrate judge and get a complaint warrant, I need you to get Cindy to sell your informant more drugs—specifically crack—and start arresting the small-time corner dealers and try to get them to flip on her. You could even try to catch Mr. Hassan with his hands in the cookie jar and see if he would be willing to turn on his boss. Bottom line is that I need more."

The Feds played a vicious game with the justice system. When they wanted you off of the streets, they would try and get you off of them forever. And if you had a crew that worked for you, then nine times out of ten if everybody got arrested, someone was going to snitch. Without a snitch, it would be much harder for them to get a conviction. Everyone would walk away free as long as people kept their mouths shut.

This problem was something that Cindy didn't have to worry about much because she wasn't out in the streets, especially since Drake had been in her life. She wasn't around people long enough for them to get to know who she was, and the people who did know her were under the impression that she fell out of the game and left everything to Hassan. That would either save Cindy or ultimately be her downfall. It all depended on which way the cards were played.

Tazz sat and waited for his new connect to show up. They were supposed to meet at Cobbs Creek Park near 62nd and Catherine Street so that they could discuss a buy, but the connect was running late which made him feel as if Hector was playing games. He had high hopes of doing business with Hector concerning selling him one or maybe even both of his nightclubs, but the prices Hector was talking about were close to nothing.

Tazz was broke, but he wasn't desperate. The one thing that he knew how to do well was hustle. Instead of selling the clubs, Hector put him onto someone he would be able to buy a couple of keys from until he got his money up enough to play with the big dogs.

Cindy pulled up and parked her truck two cars behind Tazz's red 300C and tapped her horn twice to let him know that she was there.

James was sitting in the back seat, playing the position he was meant to play in the event that anybody had plans on robbing her. Any time she was making a transaction or discussing business concerning drugs, she brought along someone who wouldn't hesitate to pull the trigger if need be. The person she felt most comfortable with was James, who was a young nigga who didn't value other people's lives, but was loyal to those whom he cared about.

The moment Tazz got out of his car, Cindy recognized his face from somewhere, but she just couldn't connect the dots. Her memory was getting bad, and she hated that she couldn't remember faces as well as she used to.

Tazz opened her passenger side door and jumped into the truck. When he saw Cindy sitting there in the driver's seat, he knew exactly who she was. Shocked, he kind of froze, thinking that she knew who he was. He hoped that he wouldn't have to reach for his gun and shoot her before she got a chance to shoot him. He was so focused on her that he didn't even notice James sitting directly behind him, and he definitely didn't see the Glock 40 that James was pointing at his back.

Before he could introduce himself, Cindy passed Tazz a small note pad and ink pen. On the first page it read, *"I don't do any talking about drugs. Whatever you want, just write it down and pass the notepad back to me."*

This took him by surprise, but he actually liked her creativity and decided to play the note game. *"What's the price for one brick of powder cocaine?"* he wrote down on the pad and passed it back to her.

"Twenty-two K," she wrote back.

"What if I was buying two of them?"

"I can give them to you for 20-K."

"Do you have a sample of what I'm buying?"

Cindy turned around and motioned for James to pass her the ounce of powder she normally brought along for those who wanted to sample her product.

This was the first time that Tazz noticed that someone was in the back seat. After retrieving the bag from James, he cracked it open, dipped his finger into it and twirled it around his mouth so that he would have an idea of how pure the coke was. Not only did it numb his mouth completely, but it also gave him an instant jolt of energy that told him it was grade A shit. *"I've got the money in the car. Are you ready right now?"* he wrote on the pad.

Cindy flipped out her cell phone and called Hassan, who was the only person besides Drake who had access to her drug stash. When it came to dealing, she only discussed the financial aspect of the business. And when it came time to deliver, she called Hassan to do all the transactions and deliveries. This was the main reason why the Feds had a hard time understanding her whole operation.

"What's good, cousin?" Hassan answered as he exited one of his crack houses in North Philly.

"Nothing much. I was wondering if you could bring me something to eat. I'm hungry as hell," she said, speaking in code.

"Yeah. What do you want?" he asked, catching on quickly that she wanted him to make a delivery.

"Can you go to the store and get me a two-piece chicken breast meal? I'm at the honeycomb," she said, still talking in code.

"Give me 45 minutes," Hassan replied, and hung up the phone.

"Meet me at the Blue Moon Hotel on 52nd Street in 45 minutes," Cindy wrote on the notepad and passed it to Tazz.

A million ideas came rushing into Tazz's head when he got out of the truck and into his car. The most important thing that came to mind was that Cindy knew Drake and probably had knowledge of where he was living. Then, the thought of just killing her entered his mind. He thought that Cindy's death would probably bring Drake out into the open. He also thought about robbing her, but he figured that would probably be harder than his idea of just killing her. In any event, he had to make the best out of the situation before he blew his opportunity to get back at the man who put him in the broke situation that he was now in. Drake's death would always be a priority in Tazz's life.

Drake sat in front of Kim's gravesite, staring off into the cloudy sky. He was thinking about what he, Kim, and the baby would be doing right now if they were alive. He hadn't been to the site for a few weeks. In his heart he was feeling guilty about being in love with Cindy, so he thought that he'd come here to seek Kim's forgiveness for moving on. He wanted Kim to know that he'd never forget about her and their child. He wanted her to understand that he wanted to be happy again, and that's what Cindy made him. He only felt bad because in reality, he was the reason that Kim and his son were dead, and there was nothing he could do to change that or bring them back. That's why it was so hard to let go.

There was only one thing left to do. The only thing that could stop most of the hurt and give him the strength to let Kim and his son rest in peace would be to kill the people involved with their deaths. Even if it meant that he had to die doing it.

Crackhead Roxi answered the front door on 28th and Christian Street, another crack house owned by Cindy and run by one of her workers named Dollar. The dirty, motor oil stained man entered the house after explaining that he wanted to smoke his stuff there so he wouldn't have to go far in case he wanted to buy more. Roxi agreed, while scheming on how she was going to get high for free.

Dollar was sitting in the back bedroom, watching TV and smoking a blunt full of haze.

"Y'all got nicks or dimes?" the man asked, standing in the living room while straightening out the crinkled one dollar bills he pulled from his sock. He watched as Roxi ran upstairs to get two dime bags, and saw that she went straight to the back room and knocked on the door before walking in. The man reached into his jacket and pulled out a gun, checking to make sure that there was a bullet in the chamber. He put it back when he heard the back room door open and saw Roxi coming back downstairs.

"Is anybody trickin'?" the man asked Roxi when she got downstairs, hoping that he could work his mojo to get upstairs and as close to the back room as possible.

"Yeah, baby, I'm doin' somethin'. You got some more money?" she asked as she handed over the two dime bags that she tapped into before she left the back room.

He reached into his pocket and pulled out some more crumpled bills that were more than enough for Roxi, who motioned for him to follow her upstairs, but on her way up, someone knocked on the front door. She was called the "runner", which meant that her only job was to answer the door, take the money upstairs, serve the fiends and scream like hell if anyone tried to rob the house. Every now and then she would suck some dick on the side to make a few extra dollars to get high with.

"Go ahead up to the front room. I'll be there in a few minutes," she told him as she headed back down the steps to answer the door.

After making a sale, Roxi went upstairs to attend to her trick, but when she got to the room she was greeted with a close-fisted punch to her temple that knocked her straight out cold. Before she could hit the floor and make a lot of noise, the culprit caught her and laid her on the bed.

The man peeked his head out of the room, looked down the short hallway and noticed the light coming from under the back door. The door had to be unlocked, because every time Roxi went to the room she would knock and then walk right in.

Roxi was beginning to come to from the punch. Fearing she would wake up screaming, he took a stick that was used as a lock for the door and cracked her upside her head, knocking her back out, but this time for a while.

He then pulled the 9-mm from his jacket and approached the back door. He knocked three times just like Roxi did, and then turned the knob. It was open, just as he thought. By the time Dollar looked up from the TV, the gun was pointed directly at his face. Even with his own gun sitting on his lap, he didn't want to take the chance of getting his head blown off for attempting to reach for it.

"I wish you would!" the gunman said, and took the gun off of Dollar's lap and placed it in his pocket.

"You can have it all!" Dollar pled while pointing to the drugs on the bed next to him and tapping his right pocket, indicating where the money was.

"How much did y'all make tonight?" the gunman asked, taking a seat on the small dresser next to the door.

"I made a little more than 1,400 so far. You can have it, dog. Please, just don't shoot me!"

"Shut up, you bitch ass nigga! I don't want ya fuckin' money or ya drugs. I want you to call ya fuckin' boss," the gunman demanded.

"Who, Hassan?" Dollar asked, confused about who the man wanted to talk to.

"You must think I'm a fuckin' joke!" the gunman said and jumped off of the dresser. "You got five seconds to get the bitch on the phone! Five… four… three… two…"

Dollar took his phone out and called Cindy on his speed dial. It was like a breath of fresh air when she answered. He quickly passed the phone to the man standing in front of him with a gun.

"He-e-e-ey, Cindy! It's been a long time, baby girl! How the hell have you been?"

"Who da fuck is this, and where the hell is Dollar at?" Cindy shot back, still unaware of who she was talking to.

"No need to get hostile. I got a bit of advice for ya dumb ass. The next time you shoot up a bathroom, make sure you kill everybody in it!"

There was silence over the phone, and the shootout in the bar came rushing back to Cindy. She knew that this had something to do with Chris. She thought about the people, who were in the bathroom when the shootout went down, and Cindy quickly realized something. The face that she recognized from the other day when the two guys shot Pooh and Hassan was of one of the men who were in the bathroom.

"You still don't know who I am," he said, breaking the silence over the phone. "It's Rob, bitch! I tried to shoot you in the back of ya head when you ran out of the bar, remember?"

"Oh! You were the dickhead I shot in the arm! Or maybe you were one of the niggas cowering in the corner, scared to death!" Cindy said, taunting Rob and forgetting all about the fact that he had called her from Dollar's cell phone.

"Or maybe I was the same nigga that blew ya worker's head off in the Chinese store... Rick!" he said sarcastically.

There was silence over the phone once again. Cindy became furious, wanting nothing more than to jump through the phone and grab him by the neck. Now, concern for Dollar raced through her mind. She didn't want anyone killed because of her. Rick's death was enough. Even though Cindy portrayed a vicious gangsta, she still had a heart. "What da fuck do you want, man?" she questioned, sounding more compliant.

"I'm glad you asked, because I got a lot of demands. Do you have a pen?" he asked jokingly but serious. "Now, I want you to keep in mind that I have no family, children or a girl, which means that I have no responsibilities. I have nothing else better to do than to use all of my time, night and day, going around killing the people who work for you. I guarantee that I will shut down every crack house you have in the city, and make every corner in South Philly so hot that you won't make a dime. I promise you that the shit I do will force you to relocate. And even if you relocate, I'ma find you and do it all over again until I catch you slippin'. And then once I catch you slippin', I'ma kill you!"

Cindy sat there and listened on the other end of the phone as Rob broke down every aspect of her drug empire that he would destroy, along with the countless people he was willing to kill in the process. She was convinced that Rob was the real deal. He wasn't faking or bluffing, and the fact that Rick was dead, Pooh and Hassan were shot and he had Dollar as a hostage right now was proof that he was about his business.

"Alright, nigga! So, what da fuck do you want?" she asked, aware of the position that Rob was in.

"You know, Chris was my best friend, and there is no amount of money that can make me feel better. But because you murdered two little girls' dad in cold blood, I want you to pay them both $1.5 million apiece. And since you also took away a mother's son, you have to give Chris' mom $1.5 million as well."

"That's it? All you want is the money?" she asked as she added up all three figures in her head, which totaled $4.5 million.

"Nah, bitch. I want you to take ya show on the road. I want you to leave. If I ever find out that you're still in the city after you pay Chris' family their blood money, we'll reset the game and start dis shit all over again."

"Look. I'll give you the money. Hell, I might even throw in a little extra. But the only way I'm leaving the city is if it's by the will of God taking my soul from my bullet-ridden corpse! If me not leaving the city ain't good enough, then I could always take the money and pay the streets $4.5 million to kill you and the rest of Chris' family."

Cindy was beginning to get upset. Rob was asking for a little too much. The only reason she was willing to pay the money was because she never knew that Chris had left behind two little girls who were too young to understand anything that was going on. One point five million apiece would put a dent in her pockets, but sometimes even bosses take losses. She was willing to accept that, only if she could kill Rob in the process.

"As soon as you get the money up, call this phone back. Ya worker won't be needing it," Rob told her, and then hung up.

Cindy dropped the phone and put her head in her hands as she sat on the edge of the bed. Before Drake could even ask her what was wrong, her phone rang again. She looked down at it to see that it was Dollar's phone number, and quickly answered, believing that it was him. "Dollar, you good?" she asked, anticipating his voice.

"Nah, bitch, dis ain't Dollar," Rob answered, and laughed into the phone at how concerned she sounded. "You got 24 hours to get the money. And just in case you think I'm playing games, ask Dollar how serious I am," he said, and tossed Dollar the phone.

"Cindy, I don't want to die!" Dollar cried into the phone. "Please, don't let me die!"

The sound of his voice begging for his life did something to her. But the sounds of two gunshots being fired on the other end of the phone made her feel even worse. She knew for a fact that Dollar was dead, and there was nothing she could have done to stop it. She looked down at the phone and saw that the signal was gone.

Drake came around to the side of the bed she was on and sat next to her. He knew that something bad had just happened. Before he could say a word, Cindy looked at him, leaned in to rest her head on his shoulder and said, "I've got a problem on my hands..."

Chapter 5

The weed smoke in the kitchen was heavy, and a quart size bottle of Henessey sat on the table, just about empty.

Rob was at the head of his class, schooling three young niggas on how to take over the world. He was drunk as hell, but understood everything he was saying despite his slurred speech.

It had been 48 hours, and Cindy still hadn't come up with the money he'd asked for. Nor did she call Dollar's cell phone to explain why. He couldn't believe how disrespectful she was in not believing the hell storm he threatened to bring.

The three young thugs sat and listened attentively while puffing on weed and loading their guns for the war. They had no idea who it was against. Rob just put the batteries in their backs and turned them up to full blast with only one thing on his mind; killing Cindy. He knew that he had the advantage on her for a couple of reasons: the main one was that he was broke. Cindy had a lot more to lose than he did, and that would make her think twice about doing certain things. A broke nigga is the worst nigga you would want to go to war with, especially a broke nigga with a lot of guns and ammo. He had everything to gain and nothing to lose by going to war.

The second advantage he had over her was that he knew more things about her than she did about him, which made him somewhat of a ghost. It would be even harder for her to war with someone she had no way of finding or pinpointing to a certain area in the neighborhood. Rob was everywhere. And even though 13th and Christian was the last known block that Chris had hustled on, that block was being run by a bunch of Jamaicans who took it over after Chris had been killed.

Rob went over the plan again, promising his new breed of shooters all the riches this war had to offer them. Taking in a deep drag of the blunt, he cocked his gun back putting a bullet in the chamber of his Barretta, snatched up one of the extra clips from the table and strapped his vest on tightly.

Tazz pulled off from the place where he and Hassan made yet another deal for a couple of bricks of cocaine.

Tazz managed to find a block in West Philly where he could sell his coke in peace without the hassle of beefing with anyone over their turf. In one week, he turned a little street called Rodman into one of West Philly's most prized drug corners.

The first two bricks he copped off of Cindy gave him the idea to make something out of nothing really fast. He took the first brick, cooked it up and brought back 46 ounces of crack that was probably the best stuff this side of the city had seen in a while. Off of each ounce, he bagged up six-hundred in nickel bags, for a total of $26,600.

Most drug dealers would have thought that he was a damn fool, but in all actuality he was hustling smart, the way he knew best. He took Rodman Street from $300 a day before he got there, to $3,000 a day within two days after selling his first flip. What he wanted to accomplish was to get every crackhead in the area to buy from him, which he did with ease. The word traveled fast when someone in the 'hood is practically giving away crack. The droves of fiends who flocked there was more than any drug dealer could imagine.

With two bricks in his car, Tazz headed to the apartment he was staying in to cook it up before his corner ran out. Suddenly, the red and blue lights flashing in his rearview mirror sent a shock wave throughout his body. He looked over at the duffel bag with the coke in it sitting in the passenger seat. He never thought the traveling distance between where he made the deal and where he was staying warranted him putting the small duffel bag in his trunk.

What Tazz didn't know—which was more important—was that the Feds had been watching Hassan, trying to link the drug connection between him and Cindy. They figured that in order to get to Cindy, they had to take Hassan down first.

This was very unfortunate for Tazz. He saw his empire crumbling before he even had a chance to rebuild it. He had hoped that the fake license he bought from the old head, Lee, was worth every bit of the $800 he paid for it.

The traffic stop was different. Looking through his rearview mirror, he could see two white men wearing suits exiting their car. The first thing that came to mind was the Feds, and the second thing was to put the car in drive and mash down on the gas, which he did as soon as the suited men got close enough to his car.

Agents Pesco and Lavinski both darted back to their car in hot pursuit of Tazz. Tazz knew the city streets like the back of his hand, especially the neighborhood, considering he used to live around there when he was much younger.

Pesco tried to call in the chase, but he couldn't give an accurate description of where he was. Tazz was taking them through countless small blocks, making it hard for him to keep up.

The chase didn't last very long. By the time Pesco turned down the seventh small block, Tazz was gone. It was as if he vanished into the night, leaving no trail behind. The agents rode around the neighborhood for a while before giving up completely. The one thing that they did manage to get was Tazz's license plate number.

DRAKE II

Cindy and Drake lay on the living room floor in front of the TV that had a burning fireplace on the screensaver, reflecting the orange flames throughout the room. It was very romantic. The only thing that covered their bodies was a fur blanket.

This was the first time that Drake had made love to Cindy. He kissed her and showed every part of her body the proper attention it truly deserved. Cindy was by far one of the sexiest women that he had ever held in his arms, and with every moment that passed, every kiss and every touch, he was falling more deeply in love with her. She was doing the impossible by helping him to love again.

The lovemaking session lasted the amount of time of two full length CDs playing. They lay on the floor, mingling in each other's juices, mesmerized by each other and the fire crackling on the TV screen.

Lying next to Cindy and leaning over her, Drake looked deeply into her eyes as he stroked his fingers through her hair while planting light kisses on her bottom lip. "What am I gonna do with you?" he asked, smiling at the sight of her eyes getting heavy.

She looked up at him and returned his smile. "You've got your hands full, Mister—"

Cindy couldn't even finish her sentence. She was interrupted by the sound of a gun being fired, with the bullet crashing through the front window, almost causing the 70-inch TV to explode when it hit. The first shot was followed by a hail of bullets that came from two different directions outside of the house. The shooters shot through the front window and through the glass patio door at the side of the house. The bullets knocked down pictures that were hanging on the walls, broke glass vases on the dining room table, and blew the feathers out of the couch right above Cindy and Drake.

Drake grabbed Cindy and tucked her under his body while waiting for the barrage of bullets to come to a halt so they could make a run for it upstairs where their guns were. Cindy's main concern was getting to little Rodney, who was asleep in her bed.

The gunfire seems like it's never going to end! Drake thought to himself while he waited for his opportunity.

For a brief moment there was total silence, and Drake helped Cindy to her feet and they both broke for the stairs. Within the next few seconds, the hail of gunfire started back up. Bullets chased them up the stairs, knocking chunks of wood out of the bannister and step, leaving a trail of bullet holes in the wall.

Once upstairs, Cindy broke for her bedroom while Drake stopped in the hallway to grab a riot pump from the closet.

Seeing that Rodney was still asleep, Cindy quickly slipped into a pair of jeans and a T-shirt. She armed herself with a seventeen shot 40-cal with hollow point bullets.

Drake was locked and loaded, already easing down the hallway towards the stairs. He couldn't see anyone, and the gunfire had ceased downstairs. The sound of screeching tires filled the air, and he knew that the assassins wouldn't get far by the time he made it to his car to chase them down. He sprang down the stairs, grabbed his pants and car keys from off the living room floor and shot out of the house, straight to his car.

When he got to the car, he could see that the gunmen had not only shot out his tires, but Cindy's as well. For a second, he thought about driving on flats, but the only thing that stopped him were the flashing police lights in the distance. He really didn't want to take the chance, even though his blood was boiling. He quickly took the 12-gauge pump back into the house, passing by Cindy who was standing in the glass door's broken frame.

"How da fuck do they know where I live?" she asked, turning around to follow Drake back upstairs.

"I don't know, but what I do know is that we need to get some stuff and get out of this house. The cops will be here any second now."

He wasn't lying. The cops were pulling up in front of the house and getting out of their cars with their guns drawn. They entered the house, identifying themselves as police officers in loud voices. Their adrenaline was pumping due to all the bullet holes everywhere. They didn't know whether the shooters were still in the house.

"Hurry up and put the guns up. I'll go talk to the police," Cindy said, and pushed Drake back into the bedroom.

"Police! Is anybody home?" an officer yelled as he slowly climbed the stairs with his gun leading the way.

"Yes… yes, I'm here!" Cindy answered, meeting the cop at the top of the stairs. "I'm sorry I didn't answer you. My son is still asleep. Everybody's okay and my husband is on the phone with the 911 operator."

"Do you mind if we look around to secure the house?" the officer asked, pretty much doing it anyway. He walked into the bedroom where Drake was sitting on the edge of the bed with the house phone in his hand.

The other officers searched the rest of the house to make sure that no one else was there.

"What happened?" the officer finally asked as he put his gun into his holster.

"Well, me, my husband and my son were asleep when we both woke up, startled by the gunshots," Cindy explained to him in her best valley girl voice.

Drake played his role well also. He told the 911 operator he called just before the first cop made it upstairs that the police had arrived.

The questions from the police officer flooded nonstop. He was suspicious about a few things that weren't sitting right with him, and he knew that there was more to the story than what Cindy was telling him but had no way of proving it. He was interrupted by another police officer who came into the bedroom and as they chatted, Cindy glanced over at Drake and shook her head, imagining what her neighbors must be thinking of all the chaos taking place.

The neighborhood watch for the townhouse complex walked the streets at night. Kids left their bikes outside unattended all day, neighbors mowed each other's lawns, and at least once a week the aroma of freshly baked pies wafted through the air. This was a neighborhood where littering was looked at like a felony. Somehow, Cindy was able to live here for the past two years without any problems... that is until tonight.

Peaches took her first steps back into the city after being in the witness protection program for the past seven months. She was placed in Marienville, Pennsylvania, smack in the middle of the Allegheny Forest. She was still trying to make herself understand why she had come back to a city where she almost lost her life, but when she saw his face, she quickly remembered why.

On the other side of the bus station she could see him as clear as day, standing by the soda machine with a black leather jacket on, blue jeans, and tan Timberlands. *Damn, he looks good!* she thought to herself as she made her way across the station.

It was more of a bittersweet moment for her standing face to face with a man whom she had almost killed. It was bitter because she didn't know what Tazz was going to do after he saw her in person since the night Drake almost killed him. The sweetness came from the baby she was carrying for seven months in her stomach that she knew belonged to Tazz, the last person she had slept with, and the only person she slept with right after her last period.

Tazz also had mixed feelings about Peaches. After all, she was part of the reason why he was in the situation he was in, and every time he thought about what had happened to him it made him want to kill everything and everybody who had anything to do with it. With Peaches though, it was a little different. While he was in her apartment, there was something about the way she looked at him when Drake told her to shoot him. That look told Tazz that she really didn't want to do it… that is, rob or kill him. She was just as shocked as he was when Drake came through the door. There was that, and the fact that she was pregnant with his child, which made it a little hard to blame her for something that Drake was the mastermind of.

"Hey," she said as she walked up to him with a sad, puppy dog look on her face.

Tazz kept one hand in his jacket pocket wrapped around the handle of a .38 snub nose, blue steel with no hammer. For the past hour and a half he'd been sitting there contemplating on what he was going to do to her if she actually came back to the city. Had she not been pregnant, he probably would have shot her on the spot. It blew his mind seeing her huge belly poking out of her sweatshirt, but he couldn't let her know it.

Peaches saw the anger in his eyes when she looked into them. But underneath the anger she could see the look of a concerned father. "Are you gonna shoot me and your daughter, or take us someplace where it's warm?" she asked with a serious look on her face.

"Oh, this is my daughter now!" Tazz shot back, being just as sarcastic as she was. The option of shooting her hadn't quite left his mind. For the past few months, he and Peaches had been talking over the phone about the whole situation, and even up until now he still didn't completely trust her, if he trusted her at all. But the advantage of her situation outweighed putting a bullet into her head.

Peaches was willing to not testify against Villain at trial, and the best thing that Tazz could have done was to keep her somewhere safe until Villain walked.

But, if the baby turned out not to be his, she wouldn't have to worry about not testifying because there was no doubt that he would kill her, and Villain would still walk away. He really didn't want to take the chance of killing his would-be first child, and a little girl at that. Every monster had a soft spot somewhere in his heart, and kids just happened to be Tazz's, mainly because he wanted one so badly.

Drake pulled into Tracy's driveway with Cindy and Lil' Rodney in the car. Tracy was expecting them, so as they drove up she was already coming out of the door with little Ryan tagging along behind her.

Right off the bat Cindy noticed that Tracy was wearing a *hijab*, a head covering for Muslim women, and the little boy behind her had on a kufi. Then Cindy looked at the house and saw that it was bigger than hers and had much better curb appeal. She never knew that Muslims lived so well, and this thought came from only seeing the outside of the house. "Where did you bring me, Drake?" she asked, curious as to who this Muslim woman was.

"This is family," he replied, and got out of the car and gave Tracy a hug. What's up, lil' man?" he playfully said, throwing soft punches at Ryan.

"As-Salaam Alaikum!" Cindy greeted after she exited the car. She knew a little bit about the religion from living in South Philly most of her life, and shocked both Tracy and Drake by the greeting.

"Wa laikum As-Salaam!" Tracy returned with a smile and cut her eyes up at Drake in approval of Cindy.

Drake really didn't see Tracy much for a couple of reasons. The main one was that she had been traveling back and forth overseas, maintaining her family business. Another reason was because he never wanted to bring his lifestyle around her and Ryan, fearing that the same thing he had gone through with losing people close to him would happen to them. It was all love when they did spend time together and it gave Drake a better understanding of who his family was.

When Cindy walked into the house she was impressed with whoever the interior decorator was. Before getting comfortable, Ryan quickly informed them that they had to remove their shoes, which everyone complied with and placed them in a designated area.

By the looks of things this girl had to be filthy rich, Cindy thought to herself as she looked up at the 15-foot ceilings with a large crystal chandelier hanging in the foyer. An all glass window that was the length of the entire wall in the living room gave a beautiful view of nature's outdoor scenery that was breathtaking in the eyes of a city dweller.

Drake knew exactly where they would be sleeping, since he had stayed there a few nights before. His room was the size of a common one-bedroom apartment, equipped with its own bathroom and a mini refrigerator.

Once in the guest bedroom, Cindy put the still sleeping Lil' Rodney onto the king-size bed. "You know that I have money, Drake. We don't have to stay out here," she said, as she took the jacket off of Rodney's limp body.

"We're in the middle of nowhere, and until I deal with our problems in the city, this is the safest place for you to be."

"Safe, huh? Drake, you must have forgotten that I'm the reason why most of the goons in Philly either retired or got on the winning team. I'm no stranger to putting in my own work. Just because you brought out the sensitive side of me, the animal in me never died. I can take care of Rob on my own."

"Cindy, you don't have to be a killa anymore. You're my girl now, and as ya man, I'ma protect you and Rodney at all costs. I swear that I will not lose you like I lost…"

The room became silent. Drake sat on the bed next to Cindy, who was staring down at Lil' Rodney. "You say that you love me, right?" he asked, getting her attention by nudging her.

"Yeah, you know that I love you, Drake. But—"

"Well, if you love me, then let me be the husband you told the police I was," he joked, but in a sense he was serious. "It's time we start thinking about our future, Cindy. And I don't mean the future of a life of crime. At some point you've gotta let it go. If you don't, you'll end up like every other gangsta in the city… dead or in jail. That little boy right there needs his mom," he said, nodding at Rodney. "Don't let him lose you too."

No one had ever said the things that Drake was saying to her. It was the reality check that Cindy needed. She couldn't see it, but her life was spiraling in a free-fall that was leading to destruction. Being 'hood rich and in charge didn't mean anything to the streets. One minute the streets love you, and the next minute they hate you, which was proven tonight. Had Cindy been standing by the TV or walking around upstairs when Rob and his boys shot up the place, Lil' Rodney probably would have been an orphan.

"Look, just let me clean up the streets. Then after that, if you still want to be a drug dealer, then at least it will be a little safer. But I really think that you should consider hanging up your guns; not just for you and Rodney, which is enough, but also for me," Drake said. He was beginning to feel the impact of his own words. He was tired of the streets, tired of shooting, tired of getting shot at, tired of robbing, and tired of just about everything. He found himself wanting to do exactly what he planned to do after Kim gave birth to his son. But just like then, there was something he had to do in order to get out of the game completely, and as long as Tazz and Villain were alive, and now adding Rob to the list, it would be impossible for him to just walk away.

In the South Side section of Philadelphia, Federal Agents Pesco and Lavinski sat in the car parked a couple of blocks away from where Hassan was staying. They had been watching him for the past two days, hoping that they would catch him in the act of making another drug deal, specifically with Tazz. Nevertheless, today was going to be roundup day for any of the local drug dealers caught on the corner.

Federal and local police teamed up and called today "Operation Shutdown". Police cars and U.S. marshals simultaneously flooded South Philly, all the way from 32nd Street to 2nd Street, pulling up on any and every known drug corner and crack house in the area. It was total chaos, and the 23rd Street crack house was first on the list.

Hassan got out of the shower and was heading to his bedroom when numerous cop cars shooting past his living room window at high speed caught his attention. This was unusual, being that it was 11:30 in the morning. He ran to his room to grab his binoculars from his dresser drawer, then shot to the third floor to get a better look at what was going on. From where he lived on 26th Street, he could see all the way down to 24th Street, and in the other direction, the length of two and a half to three blocks.

When he looked out of the window, in the distance he saw two cop cars in the middle of 25th Street, and several officers holding a few guys on the ground. Christian Street was known for getting a lot of money, and since the product that was being served out there belonged to him, he let out a gasp of air, angry that one of his corners was being raided. Little did he know, this kind of raid was happening everywhere in South Philly. Hassan looked in the opposite direction towards 28th Street, and could see other cop cars speeding up and down the streets with their lights flashing.

He turned around as if to go to his room to get dressed, but there was something that caught his eye that made him turn back to the window. "Who the hell is that?" he asked himself, looking at a Crown Victoria with smoke coming from the exhaust, indicating that someone was in the car. The car was sitting between 27th and 28th Streets. He couldn't see who was occupying it due to the tinted windows.

There was no need to look any further. He fled to his bedroom, got dressed and headed for the door. He'd be a fool to walk out of the front door with all the cops running around like they were. Also, he couldn't just stay in the house either, waiting for the police to kick in his door. He flipped open his phone and called Lil' P on 23rd

Street as he jumped over his backyard gate and headed down the alleyway. "Yo, P, holla at ya boy."

"Yo, dey raidin' da block right now, dog!" P yelled into the phone. "They're knocking down the door as we speak, bro! I'ma call you later when I get a bail!"

Hassan could hear the police in the background screaming at Lil' P to get on the ground. After a few seconds the phone went dead, and Hassan became leery of even leaving the alleyway.

He went through the contact list on his phone and called one of his workers down by 17th Street who didn't answer. He finally got a hold of Tone, one of his house workers. "Tone, what's good, baby boy?" he asked, hoping that he wasn't feeling the effects of the raid.

"Man, I'm good. Can you bring me some more stuff?" a deep voice said into the phone. "As a matter of fact, where are you? I'll come to you," the man insisted.

Hassan snatched the phone from his ear and looked down at it with a puzzled look on his face. Tone didn't sound like that, and he would never ask Hassan to bring him any stuff. Plus, Hassan just took something to him the night before that was sure to last him until the next night. There was only one explanation as to who the person on the other end of the phone was. It was the cops; probably the Narcotics Unit.

Now I'm really stuck in this alleyway. The Crown Vic sitting a couple of blocks away has to be the cops, he thought to himself as he walked deeper into the alley, not wanting to draw any attention to himself. "How the hell am I going to get out of here?" he mumbled to himself.

Police car after police car flew up and down the street. It was impossible for him to walk down the street and not be stopped, especially since one-fourth of the police in the district knew him and knew the drug activity he was into.

It was like a ray of sunshine when Hassan heard a neighbor's back door open five doors down from his house. It was Ms. Gladys putting a bag of trash into one of her cans. She was kind of cool with everyone on the block. She didn't have any complaints because Hassan kept the drug dealing off of that street. He kept it clean and quiet, just the way everyone on the block liked it. This was probably the reason why she didn't have a problem with letting him into her house, even though it seemed a little strange that he was roaming around in the alleyway.

Chapter 6

Cindy woke to the smell of beef bacon and eggs coming from downstairs, and the sound of Lil' Rodney playing with one of Ryan's toys. The sun shone through the window of the bedroom, and a light flurry of snow blanketed the ground outside. Taking another look around the room, she had to give Tracy her props on the way she had her home decorated.

After taking a quick shower and getting dressed, Cindy headed to the kitchen where the tasty aroma was coming from. "*As-Salaamu Alaikum!*" she greeted entering the kitchen with Lil' Rodney tagging along behind her.

"*Wa Alaikum As-Salaam!* I'm not sure if you eat beef or not, so I made turkey bacon too," Tracy said, bringing the food to the table.

Ryan asked Cindy, "Who's the little boy?" He had a curious but innocent look on his face as he pointed at Rodney.

"This is my son. His name is Little Rodney, and he's four years old. Say hi, Rodney," she said, nudging him.

"Amilamulam laikum," Lil' Rodney said, trying his best to greet Ryan.

Tracy, Ryan and Cindy couldn't help but chuckle, and even Rodney laughed a little.

Breakfast was huge, with Turkey bacon, beef bacon, scrambled eggs with cheese, home fries, grits, toast, cream chipped beef, and orange juice to wash everything down. Cindy could cook, but Tracy knew how to throw down. Once again, props were given to Tracy.

The only thing that was odd to Cindy was that Drake wasn't there. He had gone to sleep in the same bed as her last night, but he was nowhere in sight early that morning.

"So, what's the relationship between you and Drake? He never got a chance to tell me," Cindy asked Tracy, not picking her head up from the plate of food in front of her.

"Drake is my husband."

Cindy stopped chewing her food midway and let her fork fall on the plate. *I know dis nigga must be crazy!* she thought as she looked up at Tracy with a stunned look on her face.

Lil' Ryan busted out with the giggles, and so did Tracy, who was leaning over and tapping Ryan for laughing first.

"Oh, God! You should see the look on your face right now, girl! I can't wait to tell Derrick about this. Derrick is not really my husband. He's Ryan's big brother."

"His big brother?" Cindy asked, only aware of his younger brother, Randy, and his little sister, Melissa. "He never spoke about—"

"Why don't you two big men go eat in the living room and watch cartoons while the ladies talk?" Tracy directed the kids, not wanting them to hear their conversation. She really didn't want Ryan to hear that Derrick never talked about him. To Ryan, Derrick was the world, and although he didn't see him every day, the bond he had with him was more of a natural sibling connection.

"I'm sorry. I just didn't know…" Cindy tried to explain. "He tried to tell me…"

"It's okay. He told me all about you. He really loves you," Tracy said with a sincere look in her eyes. "I met Derrick's dad a long time under some crazy circumstances. Remind me to tell you later," she smiled. "But anyway, I fell in love with that man like I had never fallen in love before. He died right after I told him that I was pregnant with Lil' Ryan. The day that he died, I was in the hospital with him, and we both claimed our shahaddah together. Eight months later, I had Ryan Jabril Henson, Big Ryan's last and final son. A lot of people don't know that this is his son. I don't want anybody trying to hurt him. He'll be ten years old in a couple of weeks."

"I don't mean to be all up in your business, but you've got very expensive taste for a single mom," Cindy said, looking around the house. "You must have a rich husband somewhere around."

"No, you're right about the single mom thing. I tried to get married a few years ago, but I still miss Ryan. After 10 years without him, I still love that man like he was here yesterday." Her eyes started to tear up like they always did when she spoke about Ryan.

Cindy knew all too well what Tracy was going through. She never thought that anyone would be able to take Rodney's father's place. And even though she loved Drake here and now, sometimes she still thought about her first love.

"As far as my house is concerned and my expensive taste, I feel like that if I have money, why not spend it on things that I like? I inherited the family business when my father died, and now I'm one of the three largest distribution companies in America, and I just set up another branch of my company in Asia. If I wanted to live in a castle, I could afford it. I paid $350,000 for this house. It was built from the ground up. My decorating skills make it look like a million dollar home."

"Damn, girl! You're worth all that money and you don't have any security?"

"Security? I don't need any security. Hell, I can count on one hand how many people know where I live. I have another house somewhere else, and people think that's where I live. Plus, look," Tracy said, getting up from the table and waving for Cindy to follow her.

They left the kitchen and walked into another section of the house. Tracy opened up one door, then another, and then walked down a short flight of stairs where another door was. She punched a code into a keypad on the wall next to the door. The door opened and they stepped into a room that was the size of a walk-in closet. The walls contained a variety of guns, some of which Cindy had never seen before. There were .45 ACPs, 9-mm Barrettas, .40-cal Smith and Wessons, .356 Mags, P. 89 Rugers, .38 Specials, .357 Sigs, Tech .22s, 12-gauge pumps, AR 15s, .50-cal Desert Eagles, 30/30 rifles, and plenty of ammunition for every gun.

"This is all the security I need," Tracy said, and grabbed the 12-gauge pump off of the wall. "If anybody is stupid enough to come up in here with BS, they'd betta be packing breakfast, lunch, and dinner!" she said, laughing.

Cindy looked at her and thought to herself, *Oh, dis bitch got some 'hood in her!* Before she could comment on Tracy's fine collection, her phone began to ring. She wanted to ignore it, but it was Hassan. She hadn't spoken to him in a couple of days, and she needed to be tuned in with what was going on in the streets. Plus, she needed to tell him about Rob shooting up the house. "What's good, baby boy?" she answered, putting up her index finger to Tracy to let her know that she'd only be a few minutes.

"Damn, cuz! Where you been at? I been tryin' to reach out to you for a couple of days now," Hassan said. "Yo, the Feds been through here all day yesterday, locking people up, kickin' down doors, and pulling over damn near every car driving in South Philly!"

"Do you know who they're looking for?" she asked, thinking that they were coming after her.

"Nah. But they shut everything down, and counting so far, we got like eight workers locked up. Niggas ain't even tryin' to come outside right now, let alone push any work."

Cindy was so shocked at hearing that the Feds came through the city that she forgot to tell him about Rob. She had to find out who the Feds were looking for. Going to prison never crossed her mind before like it did today, and with most drug dealers who get a lot of money, it really didn't bother them until three letters got involved… FBI. There was something about the Feds that made criminals believe that they were like "America's Most Wanted". If the Feds were on your ass, it was like a step up in the average criminal world. It meant that you were somebody important enough to get the federal government's attention.

But little do people know, the Feds ain't shit. They don't care who they lock up nowadays. It can be anybody, from a crack head to a felon in possession of a firearm. Most of the time they just pick up state cases after the state has done all the work. They work like lions who send the lionesses out to hunt. Once she gets a kill, the lion comes along and takes the food. That's just how the Feds operate.

Cindy quickly hung up the phone with Hassan and immediately called her lawyer, McMonigal. If there was a warrant out for her arrest, he would be the first one to know. That's what he got paid the big bucks for. She not only had his office number, but she also had his cell phone number, house number and the number of his favorite restaurant. Before the day was over, she would know if there was a warrant out for her arrest, and it was Saturday. The type of money Cindy was kicking out guaranteed her even weekend service.

Peaches followed Tazz into the house he had on Rodman Street in West Philly. It looked just like a crack house. Although it wasn't one, the owner did smoke crack. She walked in and didn't want to touch anything, fearing she might catch something from how dirty and old the house looked.

The living room was practically empty except for a 19-inch TV that sat on two crates, a kerosene heater that sat in the middle of the floor, a cracked leather couch, and a lawn chair in front of a three-foot tall wooden coffee table. You couldn't see into the dining room or kitchen because there was a blanket hanging over the door, dividing the rooms. The only place one could go was upstairs, and that's exactly where Tazz took her.

When they got upstairs, Peaches could see that it got a little cleaner, especially when they got to Tazz's room. His room was probably the cleanest room in the house, but even still she had plenty of complaints for him. There were small sandwich bags all over, and the smell of raw cocaine in the air made her stomach queasy.

"Is this where you live?" she asked with a disgusted look on her face.

Tazz flopped down on the bed, not bothered at all about his rough living quarters. This wasn't his first time being in the 'hood, and it definitely wasn't his first time sleeping at his own stash house, dirt and all. He was back in the game knee-deep, and at this point he could care less about how he was living. Just as long as he could take a shower, put on clean underwear and use the phone, the get-back was the only thing that mattered to him. "What were you expecting? You and ya boyfriend took everything I had! And I know you didn't expect me to take you to my wife's house. She'll never let me bring you home."

"Fuck you, Tazz!" Peaches shot back and finally took a seat on the bed next to him. "I hope you don't think I'ma be raising a baby up in here," she joked, trying to break the dead mood in the room.

"Yeah, well, I'm fucked up right now, but you know a good nigga is hard to keep down."

Peaches looked around the room, still in disgust. She knew that she had the means to put Tazz back at the top of his game and help to speed up the get-back process to go from rags to riches in one day. Was he worth it? she asked herself while looking at the Pyrex pots and scales sitting in the corner of the room.

In that instant, she felt movement in her stomach from the baby shifting around. She took that as a sign of approval. "What if I told you that I had a lick that would get you all the way back in the game? Would you be willing to put the work in?" she asked, rubbing her stomach.

"What?"

"You heard me. What if I told you that I had a lick that would get you all the way back in the game? Are you willing to put the work in?"

"What could you possibly have that will get me back in the game? I lost my house, my car, my money, my wife... You know what? I really don't have much more to lose, so go ahead. Entertain me with your so-called lick," Tazz said, becoming frustrated.

The only reason Peaches was telling him this was because she didn't want her baby to want for anything. This was her first child, and just like Tazz, she didn't have a dime to her name. Being in the witness protection program and being pregnant slowed her down from doing what she did best, which was getting money. It was her future she was thinking about, and she was hoping that Tazz would last long enough in the game to be a part of it. "Well, when I was in the program—"

"Program! What program," Tazz interrupted.

"Will you just shut up and let me finish?" she said, trying to get him to be patient. "Thank you! Now, as I was saying, when I was in the 'witness protection program', they had me out in the woods in a safe house, constantly guarded by two detectives that became friendly with me over time. Anyway, I used to sneak on their computer at night, and I found a list of applications for search and seizure warrants that haven't been signed by a judge yet. The type of people that they're going after are filthy rich, kingpin types of drug dealers, viscous bank robbers, and some more people who I saw but didn't grab my attention. There were names, telephone numbers, home addresses and license plate numbers. I used to watch the

SWAT team suit up at the safe house to rehearse strategies on how they were going to execute the search warrants."

All sorts of thoughts popped up in Tazz's head while Peaches continued to explain the details. If she had access to that type of information, it wouldn't take much for him to execute a search warrant of his own, given the fact that he had to do a little extra homework himself if he was going to get into this line of work. It had been a very long time since he robbed anyone. In fact, he couldn't remember the last time he did rob somebody.

"When those cops came back to the safe house with the stuff they seized in the raids, they had everything from large amounts of drugs, stacks and stacks of cash, countless guns, cars, motorcycles, dogs, and I even saw them with a lion cub! They did all the processing at the safe house, and then transported the evidence to a facility a few miles away."

"So, what do you have in mind?" Tazz asked, wanting to hear what kind of a plan she had come up with.

"I told the detective who was on watch this weekend that I was going out to get some fresh air. He knows that I came back to the city, but he really wasn't trippin'. He told me to be back by tomorrow night, because his superior would be checking up on me then. I figure that I would go back to the safe house, sneak on the computer and get information on a few people off of it; you know, people whose applications for a search warrant that hasn't been signed by a judge yet. With that kind of information you could run down on them before the cops do. You'll know everything about them that the cops know."

Tazz looked at Peaches, amazed that she came up with all of this. She was smarter than she looked, and he wondered why she trusted him with this information. After all, she was sitting around a bunch of cops all day and night. But before he would move forward, Tazz had to get past the resentment he had towards her, and figure out what Peaches' intentions were.

Drake walked into Lora's Café on Main Street, where he was supposed to meet Tony for brunch. It had been a few years since he had seen Tony, but throughout that time, Tony always managed to keep an eye on Drake.

They had a little fallout a couple of years back when Drake refused to go to work for Tony doing the same job his father used to do. The problem Drake had was that he had no interest in being a hit man. He felt like that kind of work was for mobsters and not for a nigga that was a street runner growing up in Philly.

When Drake arrived at the restaurant, Tony was already there, drinking a cup of coffee and reading a newspaper.

After Tony noticed Drake walking up to him, he got out of his seat and gave him a hug, mainly because he hadn't seen him in a while, and for the loss of his girl and son. "So, how have you been, kid?" he asked as he sat back down in his chair. He was getting old and felt it in his legs often.

"Everything's good, Tony."

"Yeah, well, I'm sorry about what happened to Kim and the baby. You were still in a coma, so that's why I didn't see you at the funeral."

"Look, Tony. I don't want to waste any time. I've got to get right down to business," Drake said, not in the mood to discuss Kim or his child.

"Oh, business!" Tony said, leaning back in his chair in anticipation of what Drake was about to say.

"I need some help finding a guy. He's like a ghost, but worse. He has a gun and shoots at me and my crew every couple of days or so. All I got is a name, and I know that he's from South Philly, somewhere by 13th and Christian Street. His homeboy, Chris, was killed a while back, and I guess he wants revenge."

"What's the kid's name?" Tony asked, leaning forward in his chair to make sure he heard the name the first time when Drake said it.

"Rob. His name is Rob. That's all I know. If you could just tell me where I can find him I can put in my own work."

The one thing about Tony was that it didn't matter who you were or what you did for a living, he was able to find you as long as you lived in the city. After all these years, he still remained well-connected to the streets, and even at the age of 62 he hadn't stopped putting in work... that is still running his toe-tagging business. This was a nonstop business. Someone always wanted someone else dead and was willing to pay top dollar for it.

"Look, I can find this guy for you. It might take me a day or two, but rest assured, I'll deliver him to you. But kid, I need you to do something for me. It's sort of like a favor for a favor type of deal where we both make out."

Tony was up to his old tricks again. Drake knew that this wasn't going to be free, but was ready and willing to pay whatever debt he had to pay. He really didn't have any other way of finding Rob, so if that meant a favor for a favor deal, he would have to accept it. "Tony, spare me the bullshit. Just tell me what you need me to do."

"Alright, kid, you're right. I do need something done. In fact, I'm even willing to pay you for doing it for me. Before your old man died, I had a big job for him. He was supposed to kill this big time drug dealer from down da bottom… you know, in West Philly."

"So, you're telling me that you want me to kill a drug dealer in West Philly?" Drake asked, as if that wouldn't be a problem.

"No, no. That guy died years ago. But he had a kid who inherited all his money, fame, power and problems. The same people who wanted the kid's father dead now want the kid dead. The price remains the same; one million for the kid's head. I'll give you the same deal as I gave ya old man. I'll take 10%, and the rest is yours, all cash."

"This kid is worth a million?" Drake was shocked at the amount of money anyone would pay to have someone killed. "There's gotta be a catch."

"There is no catch. Try killing someone who looks out for the entire city. Practically everybody loves this kid. If you wanna do it, I'll have the intel on the kid by tonight, and by tomorrow I'll know exactly where you can find this Rob guy."

"I could care less who it is. You give me Rob by tomorrow afternoon, and I'll kill the kid by tomorrow night. Send me the info on the kid whenever you're ready," Drake said, and got up from the table and left.

Tony stared at Drake as he walked out of the door. He reminded him so much of Ryan; his attitude, the way he talked, his level of aggression and his willingness to end lives without feeling the slightest bit of remorse. But what he had in store for Drake would probably be even more than what his father would have been able to handle.

Cindy was sitting in the guestroom, waiting for her lawyer to call her back with the news of whether or not there was a warrant out for her arrest, and whether it was state or federal. Like clockwork, McMonigal called her at 8:00 p.m. sharp. She couldn't answer the phone fast enough.

"Be cool! Be cool! You don't have any warrants from the Feds or the state. Whatever is going on doesn't have anything to do with you. Call me after the weekend and

I'll know more about what's going on. In the meantime, stay out of trouble," McMonigal said, easing some of the tension that Cindy was feeling.

She hung up the phone and immediately called Drake. She hadn't heard from him all day, and despite the numerous attempts she and Tracy made, he wouldn't answer his phone. It became even more irritating to Cindy because his phone would just ring and ring until it went to voicemail. That meant that his phone was on, but either he wasn't around to answer it, or he was just sitting there watching it ring. If he was just watching the phone ring knowing that it was her calling, he'd better have a hell of a good excuse for not answering her call.

Villain stood over the toilet in his cell, working away at his dick. Lotion was everywhere, and the wall in front of him had pictures of naked women all over it. He thought he'd take this opportunity while his celly was outside at rec. Just when things were getting good and he was just about ready to bust off, a knock at the door killed the mood.

Beating ya dick was something personal to a man in prison. It required private time. You put a towel on the door so no one can see inside the room, you pick out pictures from a variety of magazines or from home who you feel like fucking that day, grab ya baby oil, Vaseline or lotion, and you take care of ya business. All in all, this is your personal time, so if it wasn't a guard at the door telling you you're getting released or ya celly outside the door getting stabbed up, there shouldn't be anyone knocking on another man's door while his towel is up.

"Vincent Thompson, pack up and head down to R&D!" the guard yelled through the door.

Pack up? Villain thought to himself as he wiped the lotion off of his hands and dick. He hurried and rushed out of the door to confirm with the correctional officer that he was being released. Extraditing him back to Virginia this time of night and on the weekend didn't sound right. The only thing he could think of and hope for was that Tazz had bailed him out. "Yo, you said pack up?" he asked the officer at the front desk as he fixed his jumper.

"Yeah. You made bail. Pack up and get ready to be transported to R&D for release."

"I don't need to pack. I'm ready to go right now," Villain said without hesitation after hearing the word, "release".

It took a few minutes for a police escort to come to the housing unit to get him, and during that time he said a couple of goodbyes to a few people that he knew, and left his celly his information and property. Then he ran to the phone to try and make one last call before he left.

It took every bit of two hours sitting in the receiving room trying to get all the paperwork done. Buses and police cars constantly brought in new people so that in itself slowed up the discharge process.

'Yo, I made bail, so why am I still sitting here?" Villain complained to one of the guards while he sat in a holding cell with another guy that was getting released.

His paperwork was being processed, and he didn't even know it. That's how things were when you got a taste of freedom sitting on the tip of your tongue. All you want to do is get the hell up out of the jail before they change their mind and keep you there. Anxious for what he had been stripped of for the past eight months, freedom was now sitting on the other side of the door that kept opening and closing with new people coming in.

"Vincent Thompson!" a guard yelled out, not sure of what cell Villain was waiting in.

"Right here!" Villain yelled and banged on the window.

It took another fifteen minutes to sign a few papers and run down his personal information, like his Social Security Number, date of birth, mother's maiden name, and so forth. Everything checked out. He was definitely Vincent Thompson.

Villain looked up at the clock. It was 8:45 p.m., and he wondered if there was anybody waiting for him. When he finally got to the door that led him out of the building, he could see that no one was there to pick him up. It really didn't matter, because he would walk home from that very spot if he had to. Fortunately, the jail gave him two bus tokens and five dollars upon his release. Hell, he was just happy to be out.

He looked up at the sky and could see the stars shining brightly. The cold night air filled his lungs, and for a split second he was stuck in a daze. The night had never looked so good and freedom never tasted so wonderful.

His daze was broken by a horn blowing from one of thc cars at the far end of the parking lot. He walked towards it, squinting his eyes to see who it was. Getting closer, he could see Tazz getting out of a black Charger. There were so many cars in the parking lot that it seemed like it took hours to get to the other side.

Villain was happy to see his boy. He got closer, and as he did he could see Tazz's smile turn into a frown with a scared look on his face. Tazz screamed, No! No!" while pointing behind Villain.

By the time Villain turned around he was staring down the barrel of a .44 Mag with the hammer cocked back.

Drake had popped up from behind one of the cars, anticipating this moment from the time that a friend at the Criminal Justice Center called him and told him that Villain had made bail that day. He'd been sitting in the parking lot ever since the sun went down, knowing about what time Villain would be released. He even saw Tazz pulling into the jail parking lot moments after he got there and almost decided to kill him right then and there, but he didn't want to draw any attention from the armed guard in the booth outside the jail.

"Look at me, nigga!" Drake demanded, unable to control the hateful glare in his eyes. "Beg me for your life!" he said, pressing the tip of the gun against Villain's cheek.

Tazz leaned back into the car to grab his gun from under the driver's seat, and by the time he lifted his head up, Drake was done with talking.

The initial blast knocked almost half of Villain's face off, and the rest of his body went limp. He fell to the ground in slow motion at Drake's feet. Drake quickly fired two more shots into the back of Villain's head, opening up his skull. He started to fire another shot, but was brought out of his trance by the sound of Tazz running across the parking lot, shooting wildly in his direction.

All the shooting got the attention of the guard in the booth who didn't hesitate for one second to pull out his own weapon while looking out into the parking lot for the person or persons doing all the shooting. "Shots fired! Shots fired! He yelled into his walkie-talkie for assistance.

Drake dipped behind the nearest car, doing his best to avoid the bullets that shattered windows and flattened tires. He wanted to get Tazz out of the way while he was there, so he pulled a Glock 9-mm from his back pocket, fired the remaining shots of the .44 Mag in Tazz's direction, and then tossed the .44 Mag next to Villain's body.

That still didn't slow Tazz down, nor did the barrage of bullets he continued to fire from his two guns.

Damn! How many bullets does dis nigga got? Drake asked himself while waiting for the opportunity when Tazz ran out of bullets.

The sounds of gunshots stopped for a second, so Drake decided to make his move. He stood up from behind the car and pointed his gun at Tazz, who was coming around the back of a car parked five cars away. He had Tazz in his sight and was ready to pull the trigger, but as soon as he was about to, he heard shots being fired from the guard behind him. One of the bullets grazed Drake's neck, forcing him to dip, get low and get out of the way. He got on the ground and crab-walked down the parking lot until he got to the curb, which wasn't that far away.

More guards came rushing out of the jail, some strapped with sub machine-guns.

Tazz stepped over his dead friend's body with only one thing on his mind… *kill Drake!* Being that he was the only person standing up, the guards shot at him when they saw that he had a gun clutched in his hand. A bullet hit him in his waist and caused him to buckle instantly to the ground. "Don't fuckin' move! Don't fuckin' move!" a guard yelled out to him as they swarmed around him. They weren't playing any games and immediately took Tazz into custody.

Drake managed to make it out of the parking lot, not caring about the stolen car he'd left behind. He boarded a city bus four blocks away.

Sitting in the back seat, he thought about what had just happened, and he couldn't understand why killing Villain didn't make him feel any better. This was the man who had shot his girl and his newborn son, as well as himself. Revenge wasn't everything he expected it to be. He thought that it would close a chapter in his life or take away the pain hidden deep down inside of him from losing his family.

Although taking Villain out didn't bring the closure Drake longed for, he was sure that Kim's mom would be pleased that the man who took her daughter's life was now in hell.

Chapter 7

Tracy and Cindy sat in the living room, drinking hot cocoa and watching the boys through the window playing in the snow outside. They spoke about the life Cindy was living. When comparing the religious aspect to that of street life, the religious lifestyle was the only one that made any sense. Cindy was a long way from becoming a Muslim like Tracy was, but she did have it in her future plans to slow down with ripping and running the streets. In fact, ever since Drake came along, she really wanted to leave the streets alone altogether and maybe settle down, invest her money into something positive and do a little traveling. There was something about having a good man by her side that made her want to live to see what tomorrow would bring.

Looking out of the window, Cindy saw Drake's car pulling into the driveway. She was relieved because she hadn't heard from him in almost two days. She thought about breaking bad on his ass and meet him at the door with a bunch of yelling and screaming, but she stayed calm, cool, and collected, wanting to hear his side of the story first before jumping to conclusions.

Drake stopped to play in the snow with the boys for a moment, and was under fire from the boys who were trying their best to hit him with snowballs.

Cindy couldn't help but to smile, even though she was mad as hell. He somehow managed to get away from the boys and into the house, but not before making a snowball to bring inside with him.

"You look a little angry," he said jokingly, standing by the entrance to the living room with the snowball behind his back. "If you're hot at me, I got something to cool you off!"

"If you hit me with that snowball, I'ma shoot you in the leg!" Cindy replied, getting up from the couch and walking towards the kitchen.

Drake went back to the front door and tossed the snowball outside, thinking to himself that Cindy might be telling the truth about shooting him in the leg. "As Salaamu Alaikum!" he said to Tracy, who was giving him a look that said that he was in trouble. She too was a little worried about him, but was happy to see that he was alright.

Drake walked into the kitchen where Cindy was washing a few dishes. He slid up behind her, wrapped his arms around her waist, and kissed her on the back of her neck. "You mad at me?" he whispered in her ear, and took her earlobe into his mouth.

"Stop, boy!" she shot back, squirming in his arms at the warm and arousing sensation of her ear being in his warm mouth. "Where the hell have you been, Drake? I've been worried sick! And why the hell do you smell like gas?"

"I know. I know. When you were calling my phone I couldn't answer it right then and there. And what are you talking about, smelling like gas?"

"You smell like gasoline and an abandoned house. Where the hell were you?" She turned to face him.

Drake did have a long night. After the situation with Villain, he went to the nightclub on 8th Street that Tazz owned and burned the entire building down. It was the beginning of a war that Drake was ready to finish. The procrastinating was over. Now that Villain was dead, there was no need to keep Tazz alive or prolong the meeting of the two.

"Look. I'll tell you everything in due time," he said, not really wanting to talk about the events of the night before. "Right now, I got to get in the shower and get some rest before I meet up with Tony in a few hours. I don't want you to worry about anything. I'ma take care of you now. I'm not going to let anybody hurt you or Rodney," he said with a sincere look in his eyes.

"Yo, you don't have to do this, babe. I got money. I can pay somebody to take care of Rob," Cindy said, now worried about Drake even more. She didn't want to lose him, just as badly as Drake didn't want to lose her.

Before she could say another word, she became nauseous and lightheaded and would have fallen to the floor if Drake wasn't there to hold her up. The first thing that came to her mind was that she was pregnant. This was the same feeling she had years ago when she first found out that she was pregnant with Rodney. "I can't be pregnant!" she mumbled to herself, knowing she was on the pill. *What the hell is this?* she thought.

"What's up wit' you?" Drake asked as he held her up, trying to get her to look into his eyes.

"Nothing. Nothing's wrong," she said. "I haven't eaten anything since yesterday, Drake. I've been worried about you."

Drake sat her down at the table. He was also aware that she was taking the pill, so he quickly ruled out pregnancy too. It was agreed upon by both of them during pillow talk that a baby wouldn't be the best thing for either one of them considering their pasts and the plans they both had for the future.

"I think it's time for me to hit the streets and handle business," Cindy said, referring to the money problems going on in South Philly. Mainly, she wanted to find and kill Rob herself for shooting up her house, especially while Rodney was there. That shit was personal, and even though she had been falling back, she still had the lioness inside of her waiting to come back out. If there were anything that could get her back into attack mode, it would be trying to kill her by shooting through her house. Until this day, she still couldn't figure out how Rob knew where she lived. That in itself added fuel to the fire.

But little did Cindy know that Drake had everything planned out… that is as long as she kept her wild ass in the house and out of the way.

Detectives Morris and Riddick had been interrogating Tazz for the past 24 hours straight. He was treated at the hospital for the gunshot wound he received in the parking lot, and was released and transported back to the police station by the two detectives. He was not charged with the murder of Villain yet, but he was held on firearms violations and attempted murder of one of the guards.

The detectives continued to ask him the same questions over and over, using scare tactics of long prison sentences to try to get him to tell them how Villain ended up dead in the parking lot. They also wanted to know who the other shooter was that got away. All Tazz would do was ask for his lawyer, which the detectives never acknowledged.

"You tell us who killed the guy in the parking lot and we'll help you out," Detective Morris offered for the hundredth time.

"Look, I already told y'all that I don't know shit! Leave me da fuck alone and go get my lawyer!" Tazz replied, irritated that they started back with the questioning.

The detectives continued to ask questions, and Tazz got so tired that he put his head down on the table, crossed his arms over his head and attempted to go to sleep despite all the yelling. For a moment he thought that he did fall asleep because of how quiet the room got. He heard the sound of a door opening and closing two times and didn't even bother to pick his head up to see what was going on.

The door opened and closed again, and this time the sound of a chair sliding across the room and landing on the other side of the table got Tazz's attention. The cologne was different than the cheap stuff the detectives had on. Whoever was sitting in front of him smelled like new money. He had to pick his head up to see who it was, and when he did he was shocked to see Federal Agents Pesco and Lavinski sitting across from him. He wished that he never picked his head up from the table.

"Rough night?" Pesco asked as he unbuttoned his suit jacket and leaned back in his chair. "Look. I'm Special Agent Pesco with the FBI, and this is my partner, Special Agent Lavinski. I'm going to shoot it straight with you, Tazz. That is what they call you, right? I know you didn't kill your friend in the parking lot the other night. The detectives outside the door here don't know this, but I do. They're sitting out there right now, trying to find a way to pin that murder on you. And if given time, they'll find a way," he explained.

Pesco was right about the detectives. They were trying to find a way to charge Tazz with the murder, but they had little to work with, considering that the gun that they took off of Tazz when they arrested him didn't match any of the bullet fragments that came from Villains' head. Not to mention that the actual gun that killed Villain was found at the scene with fingerprints on it that didn't match Tazz's. In fact, the fingerprints matched a guy who was serving a 10- to 20-year sentence upstate, having already served five years on that sentence. In the City of Philadelphia, falsifying evidence in any sort of case was the norm, especially to get fake confessions.

"I know those guys out there tried to offer you everything under the sun if you tell them what happened, but in reality, they can't do shit for you," Pesco continued in a calm voice. "The only thing they may have told the truth about is how much time you're facing. I checked it out myself. You're looking at about five to ten years for the gun by itself; 15 to 30 years for the attempted murder of the guard; and a possible life sentence if they convict you on the murder charge."

"So, what's ya point?" Tazz asked, trying to get to the meat and bones of the conversation.

Lavinski cut Tazz off and began running down the entire story about Drake and Veronica taking money out of his bank account. Lavinski knew about the robbery and how much cocaine and cash was taken. He knew about Villain killing Kim and the baby at the hospital, and trying to kill Peaches by cutting her throat. He even knew that Tazz had something to do with Veronica's death. It was no mystery how the Feds knew so much. They were the best when it came to eliciting information.

"If you know so much, why are you sitting here?" Tazz asked, now leaning back in his chair.

"Just recently, you started buying cocaine from a female by the name of Cindy. She supplies most of the drug dealers in the city and is responsible for a few murders during her time as boss."

"So, what do you want from me?"

"We don't want you, Tazz. We want the bitch and everyone else in her operation."

"Man, I don't know what you're talking about," Tazz said, looking off into another part of the room.

"Let me break this down for you, Tazz, before you start deciding whether or not you're going to play ball with us," Pesco said, and went into his briefcase and threw a couple of pieces of paper on the table. "If you're not familiar with federal law and sentencing guidelines, let me direct your attention to the charges I can bring against you; and they are guaranteed to stick."

Pesco broke down federal statute after statute, complete with very long mandatory minimum sentences, one of which carried a sentence of life in prison. The state detectives had threatened him with long prison sentences. But the difference between the state detectives and the federal agents was that the Feds made more sense on how they would make their time stick. The Feds really didn't have to do much to get a conviction, because their laws were designed to specifically target black criminals, especially those dealing with crack cocaine.

"I can make it all go away, and you can walk out of the door today. All you have to do is wear a wire and make a couple of large cocaine and crack purchases from Cindy and Hassan, the guy you bought the drugs from the night you pulled off on us. Who knows? Maybe you can get Drake out of the way as well. We know he killed Villain in that parking lot. With your help, we can put him away for life too, along with Cindy. After the two of them are gone, you tell me who's going to be the next person to run Philly," Pesco said, tantalizing Tazz with a bright future in the drug game.

It really didn't take Tazz that long to think about the offer. The last thing he wanted to do was spend the rest of his life in prison, and the thought of Peaches and the baby made the decision a little easier. The only tough pill he had trouble swallowing was the pill of being a rat. No street nigga wants to be labeled a rat. He had to convince himself that this situation was different, which was exactly what the rest of the rats do. *If they were in my shoes, they'd tell on me,* he rationalized to himself. *I'm not doing life for nobody!*

Tazz was fooling himself, even if the agents didn't respect anyone who couldn't take his own weight when they got arrested. A rat is a rat, plain and simple.

"Tell me what I need to do," Tazz agreed, putting his head back down on the table.

Drake was on his way to meet up with Tony when his phone rang. "Talk to me, big guy," Drake answered, hoping that Tony had some good news.

"Kid, I got some good news, and some bad news. Which one do you want first?" Tony asked, and stuffed his mouth with a huge bite of a double cheeseburger.

"Give me the bad news first," Drake insisted, thinking that Tony couldn't find Rob.

"The bad news is that I won't be able to meet up with you today. I got some important business to take care of and it can't wait."

"So, what's the good news?"

"The good news is that I found Rob. In fact, I know exactly where he is right now. The only problem is that I want to make sure that we still have that agreement we made. I really need that problem taken care of within the next couple of days."

At this point, Drake really didn't care what the cost would be to get his hands on Rob, either with his gun or his hands, even if it cost the price of another life. He could taste murder on the tip of his tongue, and the last person he wanted to kill this badly was Villain. The gunpowder from his last murder was still on his hands, and he was ready to kill again. "Yeah, I told you, Tony, we're cool. Just let me know who it is and I'll get it done," Drake said, anxious to find out where Rob was.

"Alright. Ya boy is staying at the Walnut Lane Apartments, number 106, B-Building. He just went inside with two other guys about fifteen minutes ago. One of my guys is out there keeping an eye on them until you get there. I'll send you a name and a picture later on tonight of the kid I need you to holla at for me."

Drake hung up the phone and raced to the expressway, heading straight for Germantown. He had begun to doubt that Tony would be able to find Rob, but Tony wasn't your average guy. He knew almost everyone in the city—that is, those who were of some importance.

It had taken Tony every bit of three hours to find out who Rob was, and another two hours to track him down to a bar he frequented at least once a day.

Drake's car couldn't have gotten to Germantown any faster than what he pushed. When he got to the Walnut Lane Apartments, the first thing he noticed was a car sitting in front of C-Building with the engine running and the driver still inside. He circled the block so that he could park in a better location, away from the apartments. His entire plan was to do exactly what they did at Cindy's house, but better. He decided to play the waiting game.

Before doing anything, Drake had to make sure that this was the right Rob so that he didn't kill the wrong person. Tony was good at what he did, but sometimes even professionals make mistakes. His way of identifying Rob could be done without jeopardizing his planned ambush.

When Drake walked past the car that was sitting in front of C-Building, the driver's side window rolled down and a voice spoke. "One guy left, but Rob and another guy are still in there." Then he rolled the window back up before the car pulled off.

At first Drake didn't think the man in the car was talking to him, but once he heard the name "Rob", he knew that this guy was most likely one of Tony's boys.

The buildings were set up kind of funny. In order to gain entrance, you had to either have a key or get buzzed in by someone in an apartment. The only thing that worked to Drake's advantage was that once inside one of the buildings, it was easy to maneuver through the hallways to get to another building. Rob was in B-Building, so he decided to go to C-Building and walk through to B-Building. After playing the buzz game with several different apartments, one tenant finally bit and buzzed Drake in.

Walking through the hallways, he could hear different things going on in almost every apartment he passed. Stereo systems, babies crying, kids playing in the hallways, televisions turned up to maximum, and the smell of several different types of cooking clouded the air.

From C-Building he could see the hallway in B-Building where Rob's apartment was. All that separated the two buildings was a short hallway and a set of double doors. Rob's hallway was right on the other side of those doors. Drake just stood there and waited for Rob to come out.

Hours passed and still no Rob.

Just when Drake was getting tired, he heard one of the doors open in Rob's hallway. Drake pulled the Glock .40-cal from his jacket pocket and quietly walked to the double doors. He stood by the doors and looked through the window. He didn't recognize the first guy that walked down the hallway, but when Rob walked past, he almost pissed on himself from excitement. He clutched his gun tighter in his hand, waiting for the two men to get a little further down the hallway. Being that they were on the second floor, there was only one way to get downstairs to ground level, and that was the staircase down another short hallway to the left of the one that Rob was walking down. As soon as they got to the end of the hallway, Drake came through the double doors and speed walked down the hallway behind them.

Rob and his friend made it to the lobby area. Rob walked over to the mailboxes and opened his to see if he had any mail. His friend teased him at the sight of the empty box, and then turned around to leave out the front door.

When Rob turned to walk out of the door, he glanced over his shoulder and saw a figure coming into the lobby from the hallway that led to A-Building. He got a better look, and just as surprised as he was, Cindy stood no more than fifteen feet in front of him, looking right at him.

Cindy didn't think that she would run into Rob like this, but she definitely wasn't willing to miss her opportunity to get her man. They both stared at each other for a split second before rushing to reach for their guns, and got them out at the same time. While Rob took the time to cock his gun back to put a bullet into the chamber, Cindy had already fired her first shot, missing Rob's head as she took cover behind the wall leading down the hallway.

Rob's friend, who was almost out of the front door, didn't realize what was going on until he heard the gunshot. It caused him to duck, spin around, and pull out his gun. They both fired in Cindy's direction, where Drake watched as she tried to avoid the barrage of bullets flying in her direction.

Drake glanced over at Cindy, caught her eye, and gave her a look as if to say, "*What the fuck are you doing here?*"

She shot a look back at him with a smirk on her face and a wink of her eye as if to say, *"I told you I'm still that bitch!"*

Drake opened the door as quietly as he could, sticking his gun out in front of him. The squeaking noise from the door's hinges got Rob's attention, alerting him to Drake and the gun pointing in his direction. Rob fired a shot at Drake, then spun around and tried to head for the front door. But as he ran, a barrage of bullets were fired by Drake, one of which struck Rob in his right shoulder and damn near knocked him off of his feet.

Rob's friend was caught off guard by the unexpected gunfire and panicked. He wanted to get out of there, but Rob was blocking the front door as he struggled to get through it, so his friend did the only thing he could do, and that was to run right down the hallway where Cindy was, hoping that he could use the emergency exit at the end of it. That wasn't too much of a bright idea. He had the right intention of shooting at Cindy as he tried to get past her, and he actually did, shooting wildly as he ran around the wall that separated the hallway from the lobby.

Cindy got low to the ground and watched as his shadow got closer. When he came around the wall, he hesitated at not seeing her standing there, but he quickly looked down to see her lying on the floor. He fired his last shot at her head while trying to avoid her gun that was pointed straight at him.

The bullet just missed Cindy's head and went through the wall behind her. She fired three shots at him, and he stumbled over her trying to get past. He wanted to try and block any bullets from hitting his face, so he covered it with his arms. One of the three bullets hit him directly under his armpit and sent a large amount of excruciating pain through his upper body. Even then, he still stayed on his feet and managed to make it down the hallway to the emergency exit. Cindy tried to shoot him in the back as he ran down the hall, but she had run out of bullets.

Rob finally made it out of the door, holding his shoulder with his left hand while still clutching the 9-mm in his right hand. He was trying his best to make it to his car, which was parked at the end of the street.

As Rob was walking down the street, Drake also finally made it out of the building after checking on Cindy.

Out of nowhere, a cop car came down the street just as Drake started jogging behind Rob, trying to catch up with him. The car caught both of their attentions. But this wasn't just a regular City of Philadelphia police car; it was a Septa-Transit police car just passing through.

The officer in the car looked over and saw Rob bleeding from his shoulder, and he noticed the gun in his hand as well. The patrol car came to a screeching halt, which made Rob start running and caused Drake to stop jogging after him. The cop took off running after Rob, and the moment that Rob tried to turn around, raise his gun, and shoot at the cop, the officer instantly fired shots.

Pow! Pow! Pow! Pow!

The rookie cop didn't waste any time, nor did he give Rob the opportunity to get one shot off. Two of the bullets missed him, but the other two were fatal; one hitting him in the mouth and the other striking him in his neck. Drake looked on from a block away as the cop did all of the dirty work.

Cindy eventually came limping out of the building. She wasn't shot, but she had twisted her ankle when she dropped to the floor in the hallway.

Drake walked back towards the building, meeting up with her in front of B-Building, all the while stuffing his gun back into his jacket. Likewise, Cindy did the same as they both walked down the street to get to their cars.

"What the fuck was you thinking?" Drake asked, putting his arm around her as they walked down the sidewalk, doing a good job at playing it off for the numerous cop cars that began flooding the block.

Cindy wasn't slow by a longshot. The minute that Drake pulled off from Tracy's house, she got into her car and followed him, knowing that he was going to lead her straight to Rob. When he went into C-Building, she went into A-Building and did pretty much the same thing that Drake did. But instead of the second floor, she staked out the first floor. Her plan worked out just as well as Drake's did, except for the initial shock of seeing Rob. "You… I was thinking about you," she responded.

Drake's phone chirped, indicating that he had a text message. It was from Tony, and even though the cops were driving up and down the street, he still answered it as he finally made it to his car.

"Meet me at the restaurant tomorrow at 5:00 p.m.," the message read.

Drake put his phone away and got into his car. Right before he was about to pull off, he looked down the street and saw the guy Rob was with being put into the back of a cop car.

Cindy saw the same thing, and was kind of upset that the guy didn't fall over and die from the gunshot he took under his arm.

Drake slowly pulled off and busted a quick U-turn to avoid going in the same direction that all the cops were in. Plus, he had to take Cindy back to her car, which was parked around the corner, so they both could escape the madness.

Chapter 8

Agent Pesco hooked up the wire to Tazz in the back of their car, getting him ready to make a deal with Hassan for five bricks of cocaine.

Tazz tried to warn the agent that Cindy's method of doing business wasn't by talking, but more so done in writing. And as of late, Hassan has been using the same method, especially since the raid on South Philly.

Pesco didn't care. He wanted a concrete case and verbal confirmation of what was being purchased. He needed it to go along with the rest of the evidence he was conjuring up. This was the way the Feds built their cases when they weren't taking cases from the State. They would build so much evidence against you that it would be almost impossible to win at a trial.

"Look. I need you to get him to talk as much as you can, Tazz. See what it will take to do business with Cindy again. Remember, money is not a problem," Agent Lavinski said as he hooked up his video camera to get the buy on film.

"Man, I really don't even want to do this shit anyway!" Tazz shot back with a disgusted look on his face as he watched the wire being placed around his waist. He hated every minute of being a rat, but this was the only thing that was keeping him out of jail. And if it weren't for Pesco and Lavinski watching his every move, he would have tried to make a break for it. In fact, that idea wasn't out of his head yet. For now, he had to play the hand that he was dealt, which was full of nothing.

"I know you don't like it, but it is what it is. You have to start thinking about you and that girl you got who's pregnant with your baby," Pesco said, looking Tazz in his eyes as if to comfort him in this situation.

Tazz got out of the agents' car, mumbling the words, "Fuck you!" He got into his own car, adjusted the mirrors and pulled off, heading only a few blocks away where he was supposed to meet Hassan.

When he got to Cobbs Creek, the normal meeting place for Hassan, Hassan was already there, sitting in a Harley Davidson F-150 pickup truck and talking on the phone.

Agents Pesco and Lavinski were already set up in position to monitor the entire transaction.

Hassan flicked his high beams to let Tazz know that there was a parking spot on his side of the street.

Tazz looked down at his waist before getting out of the car, still disgusted with what he was doing. Stupid fucks! he thought to himself as he got out. He jumped into the truck and gave Hassan a handshake before adjusting the unloaded gun on his hip that the Feds gave him to make the deal go down smoothly.

Bringing a gun to a drug deal was the norm, and seeing Tazz moving his gun around didn't bother Hassan at all. He kept his gun on his lap at all times, and was ready to squeeze at the drop of a dime. He immediately pulled out a note pad and ink pen, doing exactly what Tazz told the agents he would do.

"Damn, playboy! We been doing business for a minute now. Do we really gotta write on paper?" Tazz asked, trying to get Hassan to talk instead of writing. "What, you trying to get my autograph or somethin', so when I blow up you can prove that you know me?" he joked.

"Nah, playa. It's no disrespect. That's just how I do business. You know everybody ain't as cool as you think they are."

"Yeah, I can dig it. But I ain't everybody. My name is Tazz, nigga. If you knew who I really was, you probably wouldn't even have those kinds of thoughts about me."

Hassan looked at him hard. His gut was telling him to stick with what he'd been doing. He adopted a good system from Cindy, and up until now it kept him off the wiretaps.

The problem some of the big-time drug dealers had was trying to get familiar with the people they were supplying; especially who turned out to be snakes. Dealing with Tazz would be Hassan's first mistake, and trusting him to the point of putting down his guard would be his second mistake.

"Yeah, playa, I heard you. So, what do you want?" Hassan asked, tossing the note pad onto the dashboard.

"I'm trying to cop like five bricks of powder," Tazz replied. "But I'm trying to get them at a cheaper price than what I usually been paying. You see, I'm getting my weight up, playboy. I need you to work with me."

"Man, the best I can do for you right now is eighteen point five. You know, the more you cop, the cheaper it gets."

"Yeah, but for dat, I might as well buy it cooked up already," Tazz said, reeling Hassan in.

"Shit! If you want it hard, I can give you 36 ounces for 15-K on the nose."

"Well, I might have to holla at you about that next time I come cop from you. For now though, just let me get the five bricks of soft," Tazz said, trying to close the deal. "I got the money in my car right now, so just let me know where you want me to meet you."

"Nah, just stay right here. I'll be right back in about 20 minutes. Do you got a money machine?" Hassan asked, not really too enthused about counting 92-K in $20 bills.

"Nope so bring the machine back too." Tazz opened the door to the truck to get out. "I'ma be sitting in my car."

Hassan pulled off and raced to the stash house to get the work. On his way there, he decided to give Cindy a call to let her know what was going on. She didn't answer her phone right away, and when she did, she sounded like she was too busy to talk to him. She yelled into the phone, "Cousin, I'ma call you back in 30 minutes!" then hung up.

It took Hassan about 15 minutes to get the work and return. He pulled up and parked in his same spot, and got out of the truck with the money machine in his hand.

Everything was being recorded by Agent Lavinski, and within minutes the money was counted and the transaction was made. Hassan would be on his way to jail soon, and the bitter taste of being a rat was all over Tazz's tongue. The only people who were truly victorious that night were the Feds.

Drake walked into the restaurant at 5:00 p.m. sharp for the meeting with Tony. He was kind of in a good mood, seeing as Villain was dead and Rob met the same fate. All he wanted to do was get Tony out of the way by doing the hit. It shouldn't be hard, considering that it was only one person; not to mention the fact that a lot of money was involved; something that Drake could use right about now.

Tony was already there, as usual. But the change in his mood was the first thing that caught Drake's attention. He hadn't been around Tony long enough to know that the type of behavior that he was displaying was more of a strictly business one. He didn't even stand up to give Drake the hug he would have normally given him when they met.

One thing about Tony was that he didn't care who you were or where you were from. If you owed him anything, you wouldn't see a smile on his face until you either paid him, or he was about to kill you for not paying up.

"Damn, Tony! What's going on?" Drake asked, seeing the mean mug look on his face.

"Nothing, kid. This isn't personal, it's business," Tony replied, and pulled a folder from his black bag sitting beside his chair and tossing it onto the table in front of Drake. "I need you to get this done like yesterday, if you know what I mean."

When Drake cracked open the folder, his heart dropped to the pit of his stomach. He felt like jumping over the table and grabbing Tony by his neck and choking him to death right there on the spot. His wide eyes looked down at a large photo of Cindy getting out of her truck. He shuffled through the pictures, and every last one of them was of her. One even had her standing next to Hassan. Drake waited to see if Tony was going to say anything. He didn't know whether Tony knew about the two of them or not.

"Look, kid. I heard a lot of things about this little bitch, and she's not the kinda broad you wanna play around with," Tony said, sliding the black bag over to Drake's side of the table. "There's 100-K in the bag. You'll get the rest after she's dead."

Drake still couldn't believe what he was hearing. *If it isn't one thing, it's another*, he thought, wondering how he was going to handle this situation. There was no way possible that he would kill Cindy, not even for a million dollars. He definitely would have to kill Tony first. But thinking deeper into the situation, he realized that it wasn't Tony who wanted her dead. If he killed Tony, the hit on Cindy would just go to someone else, and there weren't too many people in the city who wouldn't kill, or at least try to kill her for a million dollars. "I ain't never killed a girl before. What's all this about?" he asked nonchalantly, closing the folder back up.

"Kid, you don't gotta play stupid. I know you're fucking the broad. You can't sit here and tell me that you got feelings for this chick," Tony said, sitting up in his chair with a confused look on his face.

Drake found it very hard to keep his cool in front of Tony, who didn't have the slightest idea of how much he loved Cindy, and Drake wasn't willing to show him. He had to find out who would be willing to pay a million to see Cindy dead. To give up that much money for one body was serious. "You know, Tony, when I walked in here and sat down, you told me this was business, right? This is business, right?" he asked with a stern look on his face.

"Yeah, kid, I told you that's all it'll ever be with me. When people want things done, they come to me and I make it happen for the right price."

"So, you're telling me that it's all about the money. You have no ties to the people you work with."

"Kid, there are only a handful of people that I give or have given my loyalty to, and every last one of them is in the grave, and that includes your old man. If you got something you wanna say, just say it!" he said aggressively, and pointed his finger at Drake with every word that came out of his mouth.

Drake sat back in his chair to allow the waitress to drop off water and breadsticks. "All I'm saying is that if it's all about the money, then I got a job for you," he said, and looked over his shoulder to make sure that the waitress was out of sight. "If you're willing to pay me a million and your cut is only 100-K, I figure that you wouldn't mind doubling the 100-K if you just tell me who is trying to kill the girl. I'll pay you 200-K for the source. Plus, you can keep the 100-K that's in the bag," he said, and pushed the bag to Tony's side of the table. "That is, if it's all about the money," he finished.

Drake caught Tony by surprise with that one. He never saw it coming. *But then again, Drake was a chip off the old block,* Tony thought to himself. He sat back in his chair and began twiddling his thumbs, trying to let everything Drake said register in his head. He stared him in the eyes and leaned forward in his chair with concern. "You love this girl, don't you?" he asked Drake, and noticed the look in his eyes.

"Yeah, Tony, that's my girl," Drake confessed. "I can't let 'em kill her."

Tony's strictly business policy was placed to the side for a minute. He thought about Ryan, Drake's dad, and how if it weren't for him, he probably wouldn't be alive right now. He owed Ryan his life, and now his son was sitting in front of him asking for a favor… a huge favor. One of his many rules was that once a hit was put out on somebody, that somebody couldn't reverse the hit under any circumstances, not even if they double, triple or even quadruple the money.

Tony continued staring into Drake's eyes. His heart had become soft at the thought of his old friend, and he couldn't muster up the ability to say no. "Look, kid. I'ma do this for you as a favor for ya old man. But this guy who wants her dead isn't the kind of guy you could just walk up and shoot without getting shot in the process. Hell, you might not even be able to get close to him," he explained.

"You let me worry about that."

"You can get killed," Tony warned.

"Nah, not me."

"This man will kill everything you love."

"Not if I kill him first."

"I don't want you to end up like your father," Tony pleaded with a sincere look in his eyes.

"It's too late for that. I *am* my father!"

And this was something that not even Tony could deny. The blood of Ryan ran through Drake's veins like a freight train, and he knew exactly the type of damage that Drake was capable of inflicting when pushed.

The one thing that Tony didn't have to worry about was receiving any retribution from Carlos for not carrying out the hit after he had already paid half up front. Drake was sure to kill him, and if he had to, he would die doing it.

Cindy sat in Tracy's kitchen, looking through boating magazines and trying to see what kind, if any, would fit her budget.

Tracy took a liking to Cindy from the beginning, most likely because she saw much of her own qualities embedded in her. Cindy had the drive to be important on a legitimate level, and she was good with numbers too. Once she put her mind to doing something, she wouldn't stop until it got done. That's the reason why Tracy offered her the opportunity to get her own legit business jumpstarted through her company.

Tracy's company supplied small businesses in just about every state in America, and in her distribution department she was missing one source of transporting her goods to certain states, and that was by boat. She needed someone to sail up and down the coastlines to deliver her product to several states all in one shot. It would save the company millions of dollars each year using this method as opposed to the continuous abuse from the hikes in gas prices and fuel for airplanes. Cindy came along at a good time, as long as she could buy a boat and get started. Tracy would help her out with everything else.

Buying the boat was just a way for Tracy to see whether or not Cindy was serious and willing to take the legal route. It would have been easy for Tracy to buy her own boat and do her own thing, but she figured that she'd give someone a chance to change their life, and help to bring jobs to their community at the same time. Plus, she had a feeling that Cindy and Drake were going to be together for a while, and maybe she could help get Drake away from the street life as well.

Cindy's phone vibrated on the table, causing her to look up from the pictures of the big boats in the magazines. It was Hassan calling. He had been trying to talk to her for the past couple of days, but was unsuccessful in getting a chance to have a lengthy conversation with her.

Tracy's home was so comfortable and relaxing that Cindy was at ease every day that she woke up. It was peaceful and quiet, and the views from every window in the house were mesmerizing. She had gotten too comfortable there, that she almost forgot about her responsibilities in the streets, and that's why Hassan was calling her. "What's good, cousin?" she answered, still flipping through the pages of the magazine.

"Ah, man, I need to see you, cuz. I'm running out of gas and I can't come to you," he replied.

The coded slang was ridiculous, so not even the Feds could keep up with certain conversations when she and Hassan spoke. It was guaranteed that they were listening right now. Running out of gas only meant that it was time to re-up, and that usually happens when Hassan got down to about ten keys. All direct buys from Carlos were done by Cindy and not by Hassan. Carlos wasn't comfortable with doing business with just anybody, especially when it came to buying hundreds of bricks at a time.

"Cousin, I'll be back in the city tomorrow. I've just been chillin' and tryin' to stay out of trouble. I do need to talk to you about something when I see you though."

"Yeah? What's dat all about?" Hassan asked, sensing a different tone in her voice.

"We'll talk about it tomorrow. Just know that it's time we start thinking about our futures, cuz. We can't get retirement checks from the streets," she said, then hung up the phone.

She was right, and Hassan had been feeling the same way lately, especially since the raid. The last place he wanted to go was to jail, and doing the kind of things he was doing and at the level he was doing them, the Feds would probably put him under the jail.

Sometimes being in the streets and getting a lot of money blinded you from the reality of your true fate if you continued to indulge in criminal activities. Hassan had heard it all the time, and the phrase, *"Criminals only end up in one or two places, and that's either dead or in jail."* That was the truth, and if he didn't start paying attention to it, he was gonna end up in one of the two.

Chapter 9

"DEA! DEA! Get ya fuckin' hands up where I can see 'em!" Tazz screamed after knocking the door off of the hinges with a battering ram.

Four other men, Black, Mark, Mizz and J, rushed in right behind him with DEA jackets on, and carrying either a 12-gauge pump or a sub machinegun. Two other men, Gus and Pop-Pop, waited outside, securing the perimeter. Their job was to deal with any unwanted guests, like legitimate law enforcement if they were to show up.

This was one of the three people that Peaches had picked out from the detective's computer when she went back to the witness protection program. It was right on time too, because the following day she was kicked out of the program because Villain was dead. That was the only reason that the DA put her in the program to begin with, and she no longer had to be protected.

The house that they were raiding was the home of a big-time meth dealer by the name of Patrick Hynes. The narcotics unit for the Pottstown Police Department had been investigating him for some time now, and had managed to set up a few large deals with him in the past. He was a major player, if not the biggest meth distributor in that city.

When Tazz and his boys entered the house, they spread out just like real cops did in a raid. Black and Mark took the downstairs, while Tazz and Mizz took the upstairs. J stayed by the door in case anyone thought about running out, which wasn't realistic seeing as it was just about four o'clock in the morning. Nobody really expected to get raided this early in the morning, and that's mainly the reason why real cops execute search warrants at this time.

Tazz got to the top of the stairs and immediately dropped to the ground, trying his best to get out of the line of fire. Patrick Hynes didn't hesitate for one second. He fired at who he thought was the DEA coming to arrest him, and waking him out of his sleep in doing so. The shots being fired by him also woke up his two children who were asleep in their room, which was right in front of Tazz at the top of the stairs.

"Stop! Stop!" Patrick's wife yelled out at him after getting out of bed. "The kids are in there! The kids are in there!" she screamed as she tried to slap him in the back of his head.

Tazz saw his opportunity and sprang down the short hallway while Patrick was trying to block his wife's hits. Before Patrick could get off another shot, he met with a shotgun blast that nearly took his leg off, but definitely immobilized him. His wife stumbled back into the bedroom when she felt some of the pellets hit her leg, and she fell back onto the bed. The 9-mm that Patrick had flew under the bed when he hit the ground.

"You stupid fuckin' prick! Didn't I say DEA?" Tazz yelled, hitting Patrick in his mouth with the butt of the shotgun that knocked out most of his front teeth. He had to stop to catch his breath for a moment. Even though he hardly did any running, Patrick had scared the shit out of him when he started shooting. Tazz didn't think that he would be that protective, being that this wasn't the stash house for all of Patrick's drugs.

Tazz wasn't big on meth, but he knew that every good drug dealer kept money where they slept. Many times, drug dealers only felt comfortable with their money stashed where they could easily count it whenever they wanted to, and that place was always home.

"I'm not going to ask you twice. All I want to know is where the money is," Tazz said in a calm voice, poking Patrick in his head with the shotgun. "Now, if you cooperate and let me get what I came for, I give you my word that I'll let you and your family live. But if you don't give me what I came for, I'ma kill everything that breathes in this house."

Patrick lay there with blood oozing out of his mouth. He didn't take Tazz seriously at first, but he quickly came to the realization that this wasn't a real DEA Agent standing in his bedroom.

His five-year-old daughter peeked her head out of her bedroom door. Seeing her father lying on the ground, she came running down the hallway, but Mizz grabbed her before she could get to him.

Black and Mark finally made it upstairs after securing the downstairs and the basement.

"Please don't hurt my baby!" Patrick's wife begged after seeing the grip that Mizz had on her daughter.

"Alright! Alright! The money is in the baby's room at the end of the hallway!" Patrick announced, sensing that things might get even more ugly.

It was fortunate that he was a drug dealer who somewhat cared about his family. In the bed with Patrick's wife lay a four-month-old infant, the one that everyone was most worried about.

Tazz grabbed Patrick by his hair and lifted him off the floor. He directed Mizz to watch the wife and daughter while he went to check the room at the end of the hall. "Don't be stupid!" Tazz told Patrick. He had to help him walk down the hallway since his leg was bleeding profusely.

When they got to the room, it looked like a brand new nursery for the baby. Everything was perfectly placed, and there was no way that money could be stashed in there because it hardly had anything in it; at least that's what Tazz thought to himself until Patrick went over to the baby's playpen. He lifted up the cushion at the bottom of it. Then he heard Tazz cock the shotgun and placed it to the back of his head while he was leaning over.

"Get up slowly," Tazz directed, fearing that there might have been a gun in the playpen.

Patrick complied and raised his hands in the air and backed up slowly. Tazz's intuition was right. Sitting on top of small stacks of money lay two .50-cal Desert Eagles. "How much is in there?" Tazz inquired curiously.

"Four-hundred-K."

"Yo-o-o!" Tazz yelled out, calling Mark and Black to the room. "I want y'all to tear this house apart. I know there has to be more here." He looked at Patrick, who was just staring down at the floor.

Cindy lay in the bed, sick to death over what Drake had explained to her about who wanted her dead. It was only yesterday that she purchased two-hundred bricks of cocaine from Carlos, and he never gave any indication that he wanted to kill her. She never knew when she inherited her father's wealth that she would be inheriting his beef as well.

For the past couple of months, D-Rock had been missing in action; that is until Cindy called his house early this morning and he answered. She explained to him that she needed to talk to him, so he decided to meet with her at her house despite the fact that it was still all shot up.

Nightfall came fast, and Cindy found herself pulling into her driveway. D-Rock was already there, standing in the doorway. If Drake had any idea that she was going to meet D-Rock, he surely would have come with her. She made no attempt to tell either him or Tracy where she was going, and only asked if they could keep an eye on Rodney for a little while.

"What's up, baby girl?" D-Rock asked as she got out of the car and headed towards the house. "What's all this about?" he asked as he looked at the house riddled with bullet holes.

"Nothing now. That problem has been taken care of," she said as she entered the house. "I wanted to meet you here so that we can talk. I know it sounds crazy, but I want to know what happed with you and my father back in the day when y'all robbed Carlos."

D-Rock took in a deep breath, wondering how Cindy found out about the robbery, seeing as there weren't too many people who knew about it. "Me and ya pops used to take a lot of money back in the day," he began. "Hell, we took more money than we did selling! I remember ya pops coming to get me and telling me that he had a job for us. You know me. That's my partner, so I couldn't turn him down. He told me that it was a big time drug dealer out in Coastville, Pennsylvania who was sweet."

"How da hell—" Cindy started to ask, but D-Rock cut her off before she could finish the question.

"Don't even ask me how ya pops found this guy. He was good at doing his homework. But anyway, we get to this guy's house and ya pops got out of the car and told me to wait there until he gave me the signal. Ya crazy ass dad climbed onto the roof, and to be honest wit' you, I don't know how he got into the house. All I know is that I looked through the window from across the street and saw a guy sitting on the couch with his newborn baby asleep in his arms. Then, I saw ya pops walk up behind him and put the gun to the back of his head. Next thing I know, I was in this guy's house where ya dad had everybody on the floor and tied up—Carlos, his wife, and his sister. He left the kids untied and held the baby in his arms while making demands."

"Carlos was a tough cookie to crack, and it wasn't until ya pops put his .357 revolver in the baby's mouth and cocked the hammer back that Carlos gave in and directed ya dad to where he kept his cocaine and his money. Ya pops never put that baby down the entire time. He thought that holding onto the baby gave him leverage, and it did, all the way up to the point when Carlos got loose from his restraints. When ya dad walked past Carlos while he was still on the floor, Carlos jumped up at him thinking that he could take the gun. I was already at the door with the two duffel bags when the gun went off."

"Oh, God!" Cindy uttered. She lowered her head, knowing what D-Rock was about to say next.

"He… he didn't mean to do it," D-Rock struggled to get it out. "The gun just went off, and the baby's body went limp in his arms. Carlos didn't even have the strength to fight anymore. He fell to his knees with the baby wrapped in his arms. I swear, he didn't mean to kill that baby!"

The room was quiet, and nothing but the sound of the wind blowing outside was heard for about a minute. It was a lot for Cindy to take in. She really didn't know how to react to her father killing Carlos' son. She could understand why he would want to kill her. The only thing that she didn't understand and wanted to know the truth about was how her father really died. D-Rock had told her that he died at the hands of some stickup kids, but everyone in the city knew, respected, and feared her dad too much for him to die like that. Plus, he was always on point. "How did my dad really die?" she asked, wondering if Carlos was involved in any way.

"I think Carlos had something to do with it, but I'm not sure. I don't think you should be worried about that right now. You should be worried about how you're gonna stay alive wit' dis cat back in the city. You know he's got a hit out for you. You need to lay low."

Cindy got up and was headed to the door, fed up with talking about the whole situation. It was as if someone hit her with a baseball bat when she thought about D-Rock's last statement. *How did he know that Carlos was in the city, and that he was trying to kill me?* She never told him anything about Carlos and the information that she had gotten from Drake. She went to turn around to ask him how he knew that Carlos was coming after her, but as soon as she turned, D-Rock's fist met the tip of her jaw, knocking her out cold.

"Where ya been?" Agent Pesco asked Tazz as he was getting into the back seat of his car.

The agents let Tazz have a little freedom once they found him to be a reliable source. He had to check in at least three times a day with an agent downtown, and under no circumstances was he allowed to leave the state. Not having such a short leash gave him the opportunity to continue doing dirt out of sight of the law just as long as he cooperated with the ongoing investigation. "I've been busy trying to get my life together. I really don't want to be in the streets forever," he answered, looking at Agent Pesco through the rearview mirror.

"So, are you ready?"

"Yeah, I'm here, ain't I?"

"Alright, smart ass. I need you to buy some crack today along with the regular order of cocaine. I want you to buy the same thing as last time, but have him cook up five bricks this time. Also, I want you to fish around and see how much it will take for you to meet up with Cindy again," Pesco instructed, hoping that he could locate Cindy's whereabouts. She'd been out of sight for the past couple of weeks.

Lavinski handed Tazz a black bag containing 100-K. The Feds had a quarter of a million dollar budget on this case, and an estimate of over three and a half million dollars in seizures of property, cars and cash from Cindy's entire organization, and that was only with her. It was as if the Feds invested a small chunk of money to get back a healthy return.

Tazz hopped out of the federal car and got into his own car. He headed for Cobbs Creek Parkway where he was supposed to meet up with Hassan in the next 25 minutes. Agent Pesco pulled off right behind Tazz, keeping a close eye on him and the money.

"Where the hell did she go?" Drake mumbled to himself as he looked out of the large window in Tracy's living room. She'd been gone for almost three hours now, and wasn't answering her phone at all.

Tracy came into the room to try and comfort Drake with words, but something inside of him felt uneasy. Any time Cindy went on a solo mission without telling him where she was going and what she would be doing, bullets always seemed to start flying.

"Can you watch Rodney for me?" he asked Tracy as he put on his jacket.

"Why? Where are you going?" she asked, concerned about what was going on.

"It's nothing… I hope. I just gotta go find Cindy. She's probably in the city, and that's the last place I want her to be.

Being thrown onto her bed woke Cindy up. Her jaw hurt like hell and her vision was still a little blurry. She could hear a voice in the room with her, and quickly realized that it was D-Rock talking to someone on his phone. She tried to move but her hands were bound with gray duct tape, along with her mouth. As her vision became clear, she could see him as plain as day, and the look he had in his eyes was creepy. After getting off his call, D-Rock began talking to her, and Cindy listened.

"You know ya pops ruined my whole life," he said, and sat on the bed next to her. "Carlos killed my sister and my son because of what ya pops did. I really didn't want to raise you, but I got to thinking that maybe when you got old enough I could have another son by ya father's offspring. But there you were, fucking by the age of fifteen, and sure enough, pregnant by nineteen. My days of trying to raise you were pretty much over, and you became a woman right before my eyes. I tried to ignore you, but damn, you looked good, especially while you were taking over the city."

D-Rock then pulled a knife from his pocket and climbed on top of Cindy, who squirmed on the bed trying to keep him off of her. He put the tip of the knife to her throat, which caused the squirming to stop.

Cindy was petrified and prayed that D-Rock wasn't going to do what she feared the most. He cut the top of her T-shirt, ripped it straight down the middle, and lifted her bra over her breasts, exposing them. He kissed her through the duct tape that covered her mouth while squeezing her breast.

Cindy cried and tried to plead with him through the tape, but he paid her no mind as he violently violated her body. He unbuttoned and snatched off her jeans while she kicked at him. He punched her numerous times in her thighs, weakening her will to struggle, and ultimately forcing her to give in. The tears flowing down her face meant nothing to him. His heart was cold, and Cindy never had a clue that he was this crazy.

D-Rock climbed back on top of her and began sucking on her titties, and used his middle finger to penetrate her. He licked her body from her breasts down to her vagina, and then began eating and sucking her pussy with the desire to see what she tasted like. While D-Rock was having his way with her, Cindy was desperately trying to free her hands from the duct tape. She wasn't sure if it was because he was rushing or just being careless but the tape wasn't secured that tightly and Cindy knew if she kept at it, she would be able to free herself.

Cindy desperately looked around the room, trying to find something to bash him upside his head with once her hands were free, but she came up short. She then tried to squirm her way out of it, but her legs hurt so much from him punching them that she could barely move them.

D-Rock finally picked his head up after leaving a mouthful of spit inside of her, and began unfastening his belt. At the sight of his dick, Cindy made one last attempt at kicking him, but froze when he made a fist and cocked it back like he was about to hit her again. He got in between her legs and rubbed his dick up and down her pussy before shoving it inside of her.

Cindy screamed behind the tape when his massive dick broke through her barrier and entered deep within her womb. It was the worst feeling she had ever felt. *How many women has he done this to?* What if he has some type of disease? These were just a few of the things that ran through her mind while D-Rock pounded on her walls. It hurt so much that all she could think about was what he planned on doing after he was finished with her.

D-Rock snatched the tape from her mouth, wanting to kiss her lips instead of the tape, and when he tried Cindy turned her head sideways in order to avoid his lips. "Kiss me, or I'll break every bone in your face!" he threatened. He grabbed her face and turned it up towards his.

"Please, stop, Rock! You're hurting me!" Cindy pleaded with tears flowing down the sides of her face. "Why are you doing this?" she asked.

"Don't talk!" he said angrily, and leaned in to kiss her despite the snot coming from her nose.

She resisted kissing him by holding her lips tightly together, but she kept her head still.

Then, a light bulb went off in her head and she remembered that when the cops came into her house after Rob shot it up, she told Drake to get rid of the guns while she temporarily distracted them. She remembered that Drake had stuffed the .45 behind the headboard, and put the 12-gauge pump under the mattress. She knew that Drake moved the shotgun before they left the house, but she couldn't remember if he moved the .45. At the angle she was lying on the bed, she couldn't see whether it was still behind the headboard.

Instead of resisting, she began to kiss D-Rock back, faking like she was starting to enjoy being raped. Her lips went soft, and they felt much better to him.

She threw her tongue into his mouth and moaned to the rhythm of his strokes, damn near making him forget that he was, in fact, raping her.

Now that she managed to free her hands, Cindy had to choose whether or not to try her luck. If she came up empty, D-Rock was surely going to kill her, and probably in the worse way. This was the moment of truth, and she would rather take her chances than continue on having her soul humiliated.

She teased D-Rock with her tongue in the hopes that he'd play the same game. She waited patiently, like a lioness stalking her prey.

It didn't take long for him to do the same, and he stuck part of his tongue into her mouth, but it wasn't enough for him. As soon as he stuck his tongue deeper into her mouth… Bam! She bit down on it with all of her might, sending him into shock. He yanked his face away, screaming at the top of his lungs in agony.

He went to reach for the knife in his pocket while at the same time Cindy scurried up the bed. She said a quick prayer, asking God to help her and begging for the gun to be there. She reached behind the headboard just as D-Rock turned back around with his knife in his hand and a mouthful of blood. *Thank God!* she thought to herself, feeling the butt of the gun behind the headboard.

D-Rock turned to spit out some of the blood coming from his tongue, and by the time he turned back around he heard the sound of something knocking up against wood. It was Cindy fumbling with the gun and pulling it from under the headboard.

Another quick prayer was said, asking God to have a bullet in the chamber, because she would only get one shot at it.

D-Rock went to cock the knife back so that he could viciously stab Cindy, but it was far too late. Cindy pointed the gun directly at his face and pulled the trigger. The hollow point bullet hit him right between his eyes and nose, knocked him backwards and splattered blood all over Cindy's face. His body fell on top of her with his pants still down by his ankles.

She quickly rolled him off of her, wanting nothing more than to shoot him again. She cried while trying to get off of the bed, but the pain in her legs kicked in, and when she tried to stand up, she fell back onto the bed that was occupied by the dead body. She just sat there, naked, with the gun in her hand, and relieved that the whole ordeal was finally over.

A good man is a man who is responsible. He takes responsibility for his own actions, and he stands by whatever he says and does. He goes down with his own ship, as opposed to bringing others down with him. If Tazz had any of these qualities mentioned, he wouldn't be sitting in Hassan's F-150, wired for sound.

This was the very problem that became an epidemic for a lot of so-called street soldiers, telling on each other in order to get a lesser sentence. But in reality, if everyone kept their mouths shut they would more than likely beat their cases. The Feds build and win 99% of their cases by guys snitching on one another.

The federal government doesn't have enough money in their budget to send thousands of cases to trial each year, so they bank on guys pleading guilty or telling on each other, because without it, they wouldn't have anything. So, many cases would be thrown out or won by the defendant if everyone made a stand and went to trial. But that will never happen. Nobody wants to stand up. Nobody wants to make the sacrifice, but everyone wants to go home.

Tazz was now in the category of those so-called street soldiers who sell themselves, their souls, their pride, and their dignity all because they aren't man enough to fight, even being at their weakest point. He sat in Hassan's truck and bought enough crack to put Hassan away for possibly the rest of his life. Tazz should be shot and killed, and buried in the sewer with the rest of the shit he lived by.

Chapter 10

Carlos walked into Tony's restaurant with a few of his goons behind him. He walked right up to the table that Tony was sitting at, grabbed a chair from another table, and took a seat right in front of him. The restaurant had a few people in it, but not many of them stuck around to see the outcome. It wasn't long before two of Tony's men came from the back and stood behind him, both with noticeable large caliber weapons at their waists.

"To what do I owe this meeting?" Tony asked, breaking the silence in the room.

"Why am I still with the same problem?" Carlos asked, looking around the restaurant at the pictures hanging on the walls. "You know, I paid you three separate times to do the same job, and it's still not taken care of. So I said, 'Fuck it! Maybe I'll pay you a visit in person to see what the problem might be.' So, here I am. What the fuck is the problem?" he asked, now looking Tony in his eyes. The aggressive tone in Carlos' voice intensified the tension that was already boiling in the room.

Tony didn't find his attitude a bit threatening. He'd never been afraid to die, and just because Carlos raised his voice a little, he wasn't convinced that he was ready to take it to the next level. "Look. I got somebody on it as we speak," Tony said, sitting back in his chair and feeling rudely interrupted by Carlos' melodramatic entrance.

"Oh? Just like you had Chris on it? He's dead, if you didn't know. Wait! What about Rob? Oh, he's dead too! And let me guess. D-Rock? Guess what? He's fuckin' dead too! Everybody you put in front of dat bitch ends up dead! Maybe I should send you next time," Carlos said jokingly, but in a very serious manner.

"You now, I really don't like your attitude, so this is what's going to happen, you fake fuckin' mobster! You're gonna get up like a gentleman, take ya fake ass body-guards and get the fuck out of my establishment before I turn the heat up in dis muthafucka! You hear what I'm saying, you disrespectful fuck." Tony told Carlos in a calm, low voice. He was irritated by the way Carlos was talking to him.

Carlos chuckled at the thought of Tony talking to him like he was a peon. His goons stood there waiting for the command. They actually wanted Carlos to press the issue, but he was smart. He knew that there was a time and place for everything, and he understood that Tony was only trying to put on a show to maintain his image.

Carlos stood up without saying a word. He just nodded to Tony, and then left. It was the best thing to do in this situation. But make no mistake, Tony's few seconds of fame weren't going to be worth what Carlos had in store for him.

It had been a couple of days since D-Rock pulled his little stunt, and Cindy was still traumatized by the entire ordeal. She had several interviews with the local homicide detectives where she lived, and every time they asked her what happened, she gave them the same story, short and sweet. She told them that D-Rock broke into her house and raped her. All of the evidence confirmed what she had told them, so there was nothing else the detectives could do but rule it as self-defense.

Drake walked into the hotel room where Cindy decided to stay for a few nights. Understandably, he knew she was not handling the rape well at all. The smell of weed was in the air, empty Patron bottles were on the nightstands, clothes were thrown all over the place, and empty food platters littered the floor. It looked like housekeeping had never been to the room since she got there.

Seeing that Cindy was nowhere in sight, he walked into the bathroom and there she was, sitting on the sink counter with a pair of blue jeans and a wifebeater on. She had a blunt in her mouth and a bottle of Patron sitting next to her. Her hair was scattered all over the place, and her skin was wrinkled from soaking in the Jacuzzi tub all day. She was at her worst, and it showed. There wasn't a woman alive who had been raped that didn't understand what she was going through.

Drake walked up to her and was about to step in between her legs as she sat on the counter, but she closed them before he could get to them. He noticed it right away and almost felt offended, but then realized that she had every reason to feel the way she felt. He just didn't want her to feel that way towards him. "It's me," he said as he softly lifted her bruised chin so that she'd look at him.

She lifted her head up, and her eyes looked like she'd cried more tears than should be allowed in one person's lifetime. It broke Drake's heart. She looked empty inside, and she couldn't seem to hold eye contact with him. She took a deep pull of the purple haze mixed with cush, and let the smoke out through her nose as she took a swig of the Patron.

Drake moved in, stepping between her legs that she opened slightly for him. Although it felt funny, she honestly needed him. He had become her rock, and the only place she ever felt safe was wrapped in his arms. She leaned forward to rest her head against his chest. He wrapped his arms around her, stroked her hair and rubbed her back while more tears flowed. Not a word was said for the next hour. Just a moment of comfort and the smell of weed clouding the air.

Federal Agents Pesco and Lavinski sat in a small office, waiting for the federal director to come in. They had a good solid case on Cindy and the rest of her organization that included phone taps, wiretaps, and controlled buys of large quantities of cocaine. Also, two out of the eight people arrested in the big sting were willing to testify against her. They had Tazz as an informant who could implicate her and/or her boyfriend in a couple of murders, and video surveillance of Cindy coming out of the 23rd Street crack house. She definitely was facing the RICO charge, which would give her a life sentence.

The federal director came into the room, and Pesco wasted no time in giving him everything that they had, including the times, dates, weight amounts, purchases and the prices charged. He gave him the names of the informants who were willing to testify, and countless wiretaps.

But, there was one thing he had trouble with proving, and that was Drake's involvement in Cindy's criminal enterprise. The only thing they might be able to prove—and that's if Tazz was willing to help—is the murder of Villain, which was a state case.

The director took his time and went through all of the information and evidence that Pesco and Lavinski had. He agreed to Cindy's, Hassan's, and about 28 more people's arrests, but he took Drake's arrest off of the table, being that there was no evidence involving him in Cindy's crew. He figured he'd leave it up to the state to solve Villain's case on their own.

Lavinski mentioned the large deal that was supposed to take place tomorrow afternoon between Tazz and Hassan and the possibility of Cindy being there, so everyone agreed that the roundup process would start then.

"FBI! FBI!" Tazz yelled, breaking down the door of a cocaine runner whom Peaches also got off of the computer.

The process was the same as last time, except this time they hit the stash house where all the drugs and money were located. The lick was kind of easy, being that no one was home.

One thing for sure was that there was coke in the house. Tazz had a good nose, and he could smell it in the air. Time was precious though, and they had less than one hour to rip the house apart. One hour was a safe amount of time that everyone agreed upon when doing these jobs.

"I want this entire house flipped," Tazz ordered as he went from the kitchen into the dining room. "Look for any secret compartments in the walls and floors. I know there's coke here. I can smell it."

He was going to rip this house open from top to bottom, remembering the extra stuff he came across in the last house. Patrick had a stash of all sorts of guns under the floor in the back room of his house. Not only did he have guns, but he also had several large packages of meth, something that Tazz had no idea how to sell, but he got rid of it anyway.

"Yo, we got company!" Gus yelled out to everyone through the walkie-talkie. This stopped everybody in their tracks.

The red and blue lights flashing in the front window of one of their fake FBI cars drew the attention of a regular patrol cop who was in the area. Washington, Pennsylvania was about six hours from Philly. The patrol cop wasn't used to being unaware of any narcotics busts, especially in the middle of the night.

"Who is it?" Black yelled back into the walkie-talkie as he walked to the front window to see who was outside.

Gus couldn't respond. The cop had pulled up to the house and was getting out of his car, along with his partner.

Pop-Pop played his part as he and Gus met the two cops on the walkway. Pop-Pop sort of had the look and spoke like a real narcotics detective, and that was probably from being arrested one too many times. He talked a good show, right up until he told them that he was a narcotics cop while he was sporting an FBI jacket.

Gus knew right away that Pop-Pop had fucked up and that he was digging a deeper hole the more he tried to clean it up.

"Keep searching! Keep searching!" Tazz ordered everyone, knowing that he was getting closer to finding the cocaine. He went to the front of the house so that he could look out of the window. He heard the police officer asking to see some ID, and when Gus acted like he was reaching for his wallet, he pulled out his gun instead, knowing that he had no other option at that point.

Gus drew his gun like he was in a western movie and fired three rapid rounds into Officer Bradley's chest, knocking him backwards to the ground.

Officer Martin drew his weapon just as quickly and returned fire at Pop-Pop, who was slow on the draw. He hit Pop-Pop in his right shoulder and spun him 180-degrees. He quickly turned to Gus, who by then took off towards the house while firing over his shoulder in Martin's direction.

When Pop-Pop came to, he tried to shoot Martin but missed. Martin turned back to him and fired another two rounds, striking him in his neck and the side of his head.

"Shots fired! Shots fired! Officer down!" Martin screamed through his walkie-talkie. "This is Officer Martin! I'm at—"

Martin didn't get the rest of his words out because Black had come out of the house to assist Gus, and shot multiple bullets from two 7-shot 9-mm Glocks in Martin's direction.

Martin didn't even realize that Bradley was lying right next to him, gasping for air. His vest stopped the three bullets Gus hit him with, but as a result it knocked the air out of him.

"I got it! I got it! Let's go!" Mark yelled as he ran down the steps with a black duffel bag hanging off his shoulder.

"Jackpot!" Tazz mumbled to himself as he pulled two small trash bags of what appeared to be money from under the living room floorboards.

Black walked up to Martin, who was trying to reload his weapon. He forced him to drop his gun and lay facedown on the ground with Bradley, who was still unable to catch his breath.

Mark, J, Mizz, and Tazz all poured out of the house, first passing Pop-Pop who lay on the ground, dead from the gunshot to his neck.

Black handcuffed Martin with his own cuffs, and then brutally kicked him in the face until he got tired.

Gus felt differently. He put the gun to Bradley's mouth as he thought about Pop-Pop who was lying dead in the grass.

"Let's go!" Tazz yelled out as he jumped into his car hoping that Gus would let the cop live. Pop-Pop and Gus had the tightest relationship out of everyone, so Tazz's hopes ran dry.

Gus turned to look into the eyes of Martin, who was lying about five feet away and staring back at him.

Gus wanted to make sure that he was watching when he pulled the trigger. The bullet exited out of the back of Bradley's head and killed him instantly. Martin cried out at the sight of it.

"Come on!" Mizz yelled, and grabbed Gus by his collar and pulled him into the car. The men pulled off in two cars, racing to get as far away from the scene as possible.

Martin pressed the button on his radio against the ground so that he could speak to the dispatcher. He could hardly get the words out as he looked into the wide-open eyes of his now dead partner. He cried over the radio, trying his best to give a description of the two cars, and in what direction they were headed.

"We're not in the clear yet," Tazz said as he turned left on Ridge Avenue. He, Mark, and J were in one car, and Gus, Black, and Mizz were in another. They could see flashing lights in their rearview mirrors heading towards Highland Avenue where Martin was still lying on the ground. It wouldn't be long before every local cop swarmed through Washington, Pennsylvania looking for a bunch of cop killers.

Tazz turned into the VA Hospital parking lot on Ridge Avenue, but Black, who was driving the other car, kept going straight down Ridge Avenue, heading towards the freeway. Tazz didn't know what to do at first, but then he came to the conclusion that it was best to ditch the car, find somewhere to hide, and stay low until the heat cooled down.

By the time Black got near the freeway, a cop spotted the car. Plus, the fact that there were three black men occupying it gave him more than enough reason to investigate. Black didn't even get a chance to pull onto the freeway before red and blue lights flashed in the rearview mirror. His heart dropped, Mizz almost shit on himself, and Gus was rolling the window down to try and get rid of the murder weapon that he stupidly kept after killing Bradley.

"Yo, pull over!" Mizz snapped, wanting to try his luck on foot as opposed to Black's driving.

Gus agreed, hoping that he could get far enough away to at least get rid of the gun. But the chances of that happening were getting slimmer as other cops joined the chase and began closing in on the car.

Black wasn't going to stop the car, but the cops had other plans. They used a technique called a "pit maneuver" that they were trained to use during high-speed chases where they clip the rear corner of the car, which causes it to spin out—only in this case, the method worked a little too much. Black spun out of control and crashed into a few parked cars.

Shaken up a little but not badly injured, he jumped

out of the car and attempted to raise his gun at the police. They fired immediately in the direction of the car, unconcerned as to whoever else was in it.

Gus tried to get out of the badly damaged car, but he couldn't since his door was pinned up against a parked car. The only other way he could get out was by using the driver's side door where Black was standing while being hit by numerous bullets.

Black stood there like he was Queen Latifah in Set it Off, firing a couple of shots at the police before being taken down by a fatal head shot.

Mizz was so scared sitting in the back seat that he didn't even attempt to shoot back at the cops. In fact, he just lay down on the floor and waited for the shooting to stop.

In the midst of all the bullets flying, Gus got hit three times—once in the hand, once in his leg, and another in the stomach. Ironically, he was able to tell the tale because he lived... something he wished had never happened.

Tony was hosting a dinner at his restaurant for a friend of his who owned a business, and decided to have a Christmas dinner for his employees. The sounds of champagne bottles popping in the air made life seem great to Tony. He was enjoying all the pleasures that money could buy.

He became even more elated when he saw her coming through the door.

His friend's "all white party" was blemished by a dark, chocolate-colored woman entering the restaurant with a black trench coat on, a black Kangol hat and a pair of black, strapless heels. She came to the center of the room and stood there while everyone stopped to stare at her. She didn't say a word, just looked around the room, scanning it to see how many people were there. Looking down at the belt that was wrapped around her trench coat, she slowly undid the bow as she stared at Tony.

The woman was very beautiful, but his initial feeling of excitement when Tony saw her walking through the door was beginning to fade. Something wasn't sitting right with him. He turned to walk away, but she stopped him in his tracks.

"Don't leave yet. The party has just begun," she said to him, and then looked over at the deejay and gave him the cue.

"Let me see you shake dem titties, pop dat pussy, do-do brown!" Uncle Luke shouted through the mic, and everybody went crazy. The stripper dropped her trench coat to the floor and began dropping it low to the ground.

Tony went and took a seat, as the Christmas party got wilder. One, five, and ten-dollar bills started flying through the air while he just sat there and smiled as the stripper backed it up on him.

The music and the yelling got so loud that Tony didn't hear or notice the hooded man coming into the restaurant. All he was paying attention to was the stripper's ass that seductively grinded on his dick. If there was one thing that could get a fat man's attention, it would be a slim woman with a G-string riding up her ass and dancing in front of him. The entire building could have caught on fire, and he still would have been sitting there with dollar bills clutched in his hands.

The hooded man reached into his jacket and pulled out a 32 shot Tech 9-mm, which got the attention of Big Reese, one of Tony's bodyguards. Big Reese tried to dart across the room in an attempt to protect Tony while pulling his .45 out along the way. Seeing this, the hooded gunman opened fire and hit Big Reese in his leg when he was about eight feet from Tony. Everyone on the dance floor dove to the ground, and the people who were eating dinner ducked under their tables.

Before the stripper got the chance to get low to the ground again, Tony grabbed her and used her as a shield as he pulled his 9-mm from the back of his waist and fired back at the gunman. Big Reese also fired at the gunman, but missed when the hooded man took cover behind one of the booths by the front door.

Tony made his biggest mistake by emptying out his clip in one wave of shooting. The gunman didn't give him a chance to even think about reloading. He jumped from behind the booth and fired six quick shots in Tony's direction. The first shot dropped the stripper Tony was using as a shield, and the next five hit Tony all over his upper body, causing him to fall to the ground.

Big Reese fired his last two remaining shots at the gunman, who began walking towards him and Tony. One bullet missed the gunman completely and hit the cash register, while the other bullet hit him in his thigh. But that didn't slow him down in the least.

Tony lay on the ground still somewhat alive, but bleeding to death. The gunman stood over him and put the Tech 9-mm an inch away from Tony's forehead. Tony now got a clear, close-up look at who the last person he'd ever see was. He never thought that Carlos would come back that same day and be standing over him with a gun to his head.

"I see that if I want something done right, I've got to do it myself," he told Tony before squeezing the trigger, adding a third eye to Tony's face.

"Don't shoot me!" Reese pleaded, forgetting all about the fact that Carlos had a hole in his leg because of him. Carlos didn't say anything. He just shot Reese in his face and backed out of the restaurant while firing the remaining shots into the ceiling before throwing the gun on the floor.

The screams of frightened women echoed through the restaurant, and it took five minutes before anyone even tried to leave, fearing that the gunman might still be outside. Tony's body lay in a puddle of blood. The man who usually got paid to do hits had just been a victim of his own work.

Chapter 11

Cindy, Drake, and Lil' Rodney were on their way to check out a few houses in Cherry Hill, New Jersey. It wasn't that Cindy didn't like staying with Tracy, because she did, but there was a thing about having your own place to call home. The house Rob and his boys shot up was now up for sale, and although Rob was dead, she didn't feel comfortable living there.

Drake drove over the Benjamin Franklin Bridge, thinking about Kim and his son, which was something that he hadn't been doing much of lately. But going to Cherry Hill made him think about Kim, and how they had planned on moving to New Jersey. He snapped out of his trance at the sound of both his and Cindy's cell phones going off at the same time.

"Hello," Cindy answered, picking up her phone first.

"Cindy, it's Brian. I'm calling you because I just received some bad news that you need to be aware of."

"Tell me, what is it, Brian?" she asked, knowing that anytime her lawyer called with bad news, someone was either going to jail or was already there.

"The Feds got an indictment out on you, Hassan, and a lot of others in your circle, with warrants pending for your arrests as we speak."

Cindy's heart dropped. All she could think about was the little boy sitting in his car seat in the back. She couldn't even register everything the lawyer was telling her, and that was mainly because Drake was yelling into his phone at someone. It seemed as though his phone call was just as bad as hers was.

"Look, Cindy. I'm not going to lie to you because you pay me very well. Off the record, my advice to you is that you need to run and enjoy your freedom for as long as you can. When and if you get caught, you already know that I and every person on my staff will be on your case, and I mean hard."

"Thanks, Brian," Cindy said in a sad voice, thinking what life she did have was now going down the drain.

"Oh, Cindy, before you hang up, I think you might want to know a few of the names of the people who are cooperating with the Feds against you," Brian said as he read through some papers on his desk. "Do you know Michael Gardner, Terrence Good or Derrick Johnson?" he asked rhetorically, not really needing an answer. Then he hung up the phone.

Damn, Rick! You were cooperating? Cindy asked herself about her dead friend. She had no idea who Terrance or Michael was, but what she did know was that setting foot back in Philly was a no-no.

Drake hung up his phone, mad about the news he just heard. "Tony's dead—"

"The Feds indicted me—"

They spoke at the same time, and turned to face one another.

Drake pulled the car over immediately after exiting the bridge. He didn't know whose news was the worst at first, but he quickly came to the realization that it was Cindy's. He could see the hurt in her eyes—the kind of hurt he never saw before.

"I don't even know any damn Terrance Good or Michael Gardner!" she said, and put her face in her hands.

The name Terrance Good sent chills down Drake's spine. He knew exactly whose name that was when he and Veronica cleaned out Tazz's bank account. It was one of the many things he had to remember in order to gain access to the account. "You're telling me that you don't know who Terrance is?" he questioned, looking at her strangely, and thinking about all the long conversations they had about him and Villain.

"Who the hell is he?"

"Terrance is Tazz, Cindy!"

"Tazz? Oh, shit! That Tazz!" she said, shocked. Although Cindy never knew his government name she couldn't believe she had slipped and hadn't put two and two together. She also remembered that Carlos had set up the first deal with him and that's why Cindy never worried if he was legit.

She immediately got on her phone to call Hassan, wanting to warn him about Tazz. She couldn't believe that she didn't recognize his face from the courtroom, and here she was, dealing with the enemy who was also a rat. She felt bad, and as Hassan's phone rang, she couldn't even begin to look at Drake, who was still trying to process the whole ordeal.

Tazz had a long night, but he, Mark, and J pulled back into the city around nine in the morning. His idea of taking their chances on foot had paid off.

After leaving the car in the VA Hospital parking lot, they met up with a fat black guy who was sitting on the porch with his girlfriend, smoking weed. The fat nigga, named Dirty, almost shot all three of them when they came walking down the street. Tazz didn't even know that he was in the 'hood when he walked up Erie Avenue, but Dirty definitely informed him when the sound of his gun cocking caught their attention.

After listening to Tazz briefly explain his situation, not only did Dirty take them in off of the streets, he also provided them with a ride back to Philly, free of charge. Dirty hated cops and he loved gangstas. He sold drugs, and he also put in work just like Tazz and them. If he had been in their shoes, he would have wanted someone to help him out too. It was more like an "honor amongst thieves" type of situation.

It was early in the morning, and Tazz had his day cut out for him. He had to immediately call Agent Pesco to let him know that he was ready to work. Then, he had to contact Hassan to set up the deal. All this was done within one hour of being back in the city.

That was just how fast a crud-ball could work. There was no task that a slimy nigga wouldn't do, especially if he's trying to stay out of jail, and Tazz was no exception. He was one of the worst kind of shiesty niggas. He'd bust his gun, and he'd get you locked up.

By noon, every federal agent, U.S. Marshal and local police officer was in position, ready to carry out what was called "Operation Dead Zone". The only snag was that they had no idea where Cindy was. Although that was a problem, it didn't stop the show.

Tazz pulled into the Burger King parking lot where Hassan told him to meet him. Hassan was sitting in his truck with the engine running, like always. Tazz got out of his car, looked around, then headed to the passenger side of Hassan's truck. Once inside, business was conducted as usual, at least in Tazz's eyes.

"Damn, homie! You played me out!" Hassan said as he looked out of the window at the cars riding up and down the street, and also at the cars in the parking lot.

"Fuck is you talking about?" Tazz asked and chuckled, trying his best to fake it.

Hassan took another look around the parking lot and pinned his eyes on a car that was sitting there when he arrived, but just decided to turn the engine on. He never got a chance to see who was in the car because they never got out. But he knew exactly who it was. He pulled his gun from under his jacket and pointed it at Tazz while he maintained a close eye on the blue Crown Victoria in front of him.

Tazz couldn't get a word out before Hassan squeezed the trigger, and then slammed the truck into drive. Two quick shells hit him in his side, and he tried his best to get out of the way of any more hot shit that might be flying his way.

Hassan stepped on the gas and pushed it to the floor, racing to make it past the exit that was only about twenty yards away. The acceleration pushed Tazz backwards, making it difficult for him to get the door open.

As Hassan raced towards the exit, he squeezed off three more shots from under his right arm, which was steering the truck. One bullet missed Tazz and shattered the window, but the other two hit him in his face and head, splattering blood and brain matter all over the passenger side window. "That's for Cindy and Drake, you rat ass bitch!" Hassan mumbled to himself as he glanced over at Tazz's body that was slumped over in the seat.

When he turned his head back towards the exit, he saw a cop car trying to block it. The cop car wasn't big enough to block it alone, so Hassan crashed the F-150 into the back of it, spinning it away from the exit.

The federal agents in the Crown Victoria opened fire at the truck, trying their best to neutralize Hassan before he got a chance to hurt anyone else, but Hassan's truck was built tough.

The truck screeched out onto 58th Street, sideswiping a few cars in the process. Agents and cop cars followed him through the streets, and for a large truck, Hassan had a vicious whip game. He pushed cars through red lights, drove onto the pavement, and even struck a girl who was attempting to cross the street. He was trying everything to get away, and for a moment it looked as though he would when the cops backed off from him. The only reason they did that was to prevent any more major accidents as he sped through the crowded city streets. They wanted to keep civilian casualties to a limit.

Hassan turned off of 58th Street and headed down Chestnut Street where there were three lanes that headed straight for the downtown area. He leaned over Tazz's dead body, opened the glove compartment, and grabbed a CD. You would think that he would want to listen to some ride or die music, but instead, he popped in James Brown. "This is a Man's World" flooded the speakers.

He looked into his rearview mirror and could see that the cops were back on his tail. He grabbed his phone and dialed Cindy's number, wanting to hear a familiar voice before his time was up.

"Yo, cuz! Where you at?" she answered the phone when she saw his number pop up on the screen.

"Hey, cousin. I took care of part of your problem," he said, looking over at Tazz's dead body. "I can't talk long because the cops are chasing me right now. I just wanted to let you know that I love you, baby girl. You take good care of Lil' Rodney, and keep Drake out of trouble."

"Cousin, you don't have to do this!" Cindy pleaded, feeling that Hassan was about to do something that might cost him his life.

"Nah, cousin. It's over for me."

"Where are you?"

"I got to go—"

"Hassan... Hassan!"

The phone went dead in Cindy's ear because one of the cop cars had slammed into the back of Hassan's truck, causing him to spin out. The left tires gave out when all of the weight shifted to that side, which caused the truck to overturn. It tumbled over and over again for about 25 yards before coming to a stop. Tazz's body flew out of the passenger side window during the process.

Ironically, Hassan was still alive but pinned between the steering wheel and the smashed-in door. His truck landed on the corner of 40th and Chestnut Street, right in front of the entrance to a bank. His leg was banged up pretty good, and the impact from the airbag busted his mouth up too. But all he could do was think about getting out of the truck before the cops got there.

When he heard a cop yell out, "He's got a gun! He's got a gun! Put the gun down! Put the gun down!" he knew that it was over for him, especially since he didn't have a gun in his hand. The only thing that saved him from dying by gunfire was the fact that his truck started smoking. Then, there was a small explosion that caused the truck to go up in flames.

Hassan was trapped inside, and the only thing that could keep him from being burnt alive was his smashed-in door that was pinned between the sidewalk and a sewer drain gate. All he could think about was the fire that quickly made its way into the truck cab.

Cindy's many futile attempts at calling Hassan back were denied by his phone going straight to voicemail. She and Drake rushed back to Tracy's house in order to grab a few things—mainly money—because she was officially a wanted woman. The money she had in the bank was frozen by the Feds, so all she could rely on was the money that she had on the streets, the money she had at Tracy's, and the money she had put up for a rainy day and/or in case of an emergency.

She thought about every dime that she had access to, which was about $1.5 million, and that included the one million in cash she had stashed at her old house. That was more than enough money to go on the run with for a few years, or at least for seven years to guarantee that the statue of limitations would run out on her indictment. "I've got to get to the house so I can get my money," she told Drake as he pulled into Tracy's driveway. "I got enough money to keep us cool for a while."

Drake looked at her like she was crazy. "You can't go back to the house, Cindy. Don't you think that's the first place the Feds are going to look for you? Come on, babe. You gotta be a little smarter than that if you plan on being on the run," he told her.

"Well, how far do you think we can get on 100-K?" she snapped back. "I got 400-K worth of drugs on the streets that I can't collect right now, and it's possible that Hassan is either dead or in jail, so most of that is gone with him!"

"Shh! Damn, babe! You're worrying too much," he said, trying to calm her down. "Didn't I tell you that I was going to hold you down no matter what?" He walked up behind her in the driveway. "I got some money put up. There's a little more than a million. I figure that it should last for a while until I get a job." He chuckled at the idea of working a nine to five. "I'm not going to lose you. All I need for you to do is put your trust in me just this one time."

"I trust you. I just don't want to leave behind anything that's going to give me a reason to come back."

"What's going to tempt you to come back to a place that wants you dead?"

"I have a million in cash at the house, and if the Feds do go there, I know for sure that they might find it."

"I don't know, Cindy. It sounds too dangerous."

"Baby, we can use the money. There's no limit to how much we'll need being on the run. Just think about it before we leave it behind," she said, wanting only to hear him say yes to her request.

"So, who's supposed to be going to get the money?" Drake asked with a raised eyebrow.

"You can go get it. The Feds don't have a warrant out for you, nor are you on the indictment. Brian told me that when he called me earlier."

"Brian told you that?" he asked suspiciously.

"Yeah. I'm not going to lie to you. Here, call, and ask him yourself," she said, and pulled her phone out of her pocket and stuck it in his face.

As she held the phone it began to ring. She looked at the screen, hoping to see Hassan's number, but it turned out to be Carlos. She was shocked that he had the audacity to call her after trying to have her killed. At first she wasn't going to answer it, but curiosity got the best of her. She had to know what his reason was for calling, so she answered it but didn't say a word.

"Cinde-e-e-e!" Carlos whispered into the phone in a creepy voice. "I know you're listening, and you don't have to say anything." He went back to his regular voice and laughed to himself about how creepy he sounded. "I guess you already know by now that I'm trying my best to kill you. And if you don't know... well... you damn sure know now! I can go into all the reasons why I want you dead, but that would just be a waste of my time."

"What da fuck do you want, Carlos?" Cindy said, irritated by the sound of his voice.

"Aw! There she goes!" he said, happy to hear her

voice. "Look. I'm glad you asked that, because I've got a proposition for you that you might want to hear."

"Yeah? What's that?"

"I'll trade you two lives for the price of one. And before you ask, I'll just give you the names to save time. I'll trade you the lives of Drake and your son, Rodney, for your life."

Cindy didn't know what to make of that statement at first. She spun around and scanned the area well to see if anything looked suspicious or out of the norm. Carlos did have a boatload of money, so it would mean nothing for him to pay someone to find and follow her back to Tracy's house.

"Look, Cindy. You can either let me kill you, or let the Feds kill you, 'cause as soon as they get their hands on your pretty little black ass, you're going away for life."

She thought about what he was saying, and in a sense he was sort of right about the Feds. She was definitely looking at a life sentence, unless she became a rat, and the chance of that equaled the chance of a man getting pregnant with twins. Carlos was one loose end she couldn't afford to leave behind. As long as he was alive, she would always live in fear.

"I've got a better idea," Cindy proposed, thinking of a way to cut into his pride. "How about me and you meet up somewhere by ourselves and shoot at each other until somebody dies?"

"O-o-o-oh! Take ten paces, then turn and squeeze the trigger!" he said, going back to his creepy voice. "That sounds like a plan, but how do I know you're going to come alone?"

"Because I'm not afraid of you. Whether you come alone or bring your whole crew, I'ma be there with a big gun and a lot of bullets."

Her plan was working just as she expected it. The one thing any real man can't stand is a woman overpowering him. It's just a part of a guy's DNA.

Carlos was hot under the collar and irritated at the thought of her challenging him. More importantly, he knew that she was crazy enough to do it. "Alright, little lady. Where do you want to meet up?" he asked, accepting the face-off.

"I'll call you back in 10 minutes to let you know. Oh, and Carlos, please don't bitch-up when it's time to go to work. The worst thing any man could do is be a coward," she said, then hung up on him.

"You must be out of ya got damn mind, Cindy!" Drake declared, grabbing her by her shoulders.

He didn't understand how tired she was with dealing with the whole situation. In fact, she was just plain old tired of everything. With D-Rock raping her, Rob trying to kill her, the Feds having a warrant out for her arrest, and last but not least, Carlos wanting nothing else but to see her dead, it was too much for her to handle. She only knew one way to deal with Carlos, and that was to kill him even if it meant her dying in the process.

It was times like these that she lost focus on other important things in her life, like Lil' Rodney. Her mind was made up, and there was nothing anybody could do or say that would keep her from confronting Carlos before she, Lil' Rodney, and Drake left town for good.

The fire department truck arrived on 40th and Chestnut Street from the fire station located on 43rd and Market, to put out the blazing truck. There was not one cop willing to get near the fire to try and rescue Hassan. They just stood there at a distance and watched the truck burn. The Feds knew for sure that Hassan was dead, which was something they really weren't concerned about, just as long as he was off of the streets.

After the fire was mostly out, Pesco ran over to the truck hoping to see Hassan's badly charred body. But when he got there, the truck was completely empty, and for a second he thought that he was tripping. He walked around the truck and looked through all of the windows, and still, there was nothing. He took a closer look at the driver's side door and saw that the grille to a sewer hole had been removed. The truck had landed at an angle where Hassan could have climbed out of the window and straight into the sewer hole despite the door being crushed in. "Flip the truck over! Flip the truck over!" Pesco yelled at the firemen, thinking that Hassan had to be in the sewer. The firemen rushed over to the truck and all together they pushed it back over onto its wheels.

Pesco looked into the sewer and could see a pipeline that was big enough for someone to go through. That was enough to send him into a panic. "I want a layout of this sewer system! I want an officer standing over every storm drain within a 15-block radius! I wanna know where this storm drain leads to, and I wanna know now!" he yelled, and clapped his hands angrily in order to get people moving faster. "Somebody get this truck out of here! Get it down to the lab for processing!" he commanded.

The scene was chaotic, and the manhunt for Hassan was immediate. News cameras and reporters were on the scene, and a crowd of people filled the pavement, wondering what in the hell was going on. Traffic was backed up for several blocks, and the horns of enraged drivers sounded off. The quicker they could remove the truck, the quicker traffic could get back to normal.

The only question that was on Pesco's mind was, *Where in the hell did Hassan go?*

Chapter 12

"I'ma be fine," Cindy told Drake as she stood in the mirror and strapped the bulletproof vest to her chest. Cindy acted like this was routine for her. It seemed as though she didn't have a worry in the world, and that bothered the hell out of Drake. He just sat on the bed and watched her as she walked around the room, loading her extra clips and cleaning out the barrel of her two Glock 40s.

"Cindy, you don't have to do this," Drake said in a low tone, trying his best to stay cool. He wanted nothing more than to stop her from doing what she was about to do. He said everything he could say to prevent her from going; even offering to go in her place. But nothing was getting through to her. Her mind was already made up.

"Look. I trust you to go get the million from the house. Now, I also need you to trust me when I say that I'll be home in about two hours. After that, I promise you that you can take me wherever you want to go, and I'll do whatever you want me to do. Just let me take care of my business first."

"We can leave right now, Cindy. I'll even go get the money from the house, and we can just hit the road. Fuck Carlos!"

Cindy knelt down in front of him. "I know it's hard trying to be a man when ya woman's got a set of balls just as big as yours," she said with a smile, trying to get Drake to do the same. "Babe, look at me. I've been doing shit like this before you met me, and I thank God that you came along and saved me. But just try to put yourself in my shoes and ask yourself what you would do."

Tracy didn't want to interrupt, but she busted into the room, grabbed the remote control off of the bed and turned on the TV. "Do y'all know this guy?" she asked, flicking to the news station and turning the volume up.

As clear as day, Hassan's face popped up on the screen. The news anchor presented breaking news about a manhunt that was underway in West Philadelphia, with Hassan being the center of attention.

Cindy, Drake, and Tracy just stared at the television in amazement at how badly the truck had crashed and burned, and was now being hauled off on a flatbed truck.

"*...He's considered armed and dangerous. If you see this man, call the police right away...*" the female news anchor said before switching to another story.

Cindy immediately tried to call Hassan's cell phone, but as expected, it went straight to voicemail. It was a relief for her to see that Hassan had gotten away, but she was more concerned about whether or not he was physically okay.

You had to have been a Houdini to get out of some shit like that! Drake thought to himself.

"Look. I got to go," Cindy said, and grabbed her coat from the closet and her guns from off of the dresser.

Just then, Lil' Rodney and Ryan ran into the room. Rodney ran to Cindy and wrapped his arms around her legs and laughed at Ryan, who was chasing him. She picked him up and gave him a big hug, not knowing if she would ever see him again, but trying her best not to think about it. He was so innocent and pure. He had no idea what was going on, but everyone else in the room did. Tracy had to leave because the sight of Cindy holding onto her son the way she did made her shed a few tears.

Drake tried his best to play it cool, but as soon as Lil' Rodney said, "Mommy, where are you going?" his eyes watered up also, and he stormed out of the room, disgusted with Cindy.

Even gangstas have feelings, and Drake was finally starting to realize that too, all at the hands of a four-year old.

The flatbed truck with Hassan's truck on it was being taken to the Federal Building downtown on 6th and

Market Street to be processed and a police escort led the way. As they crossed over onto 30th Street, a metal plate dropped from underneath Hassan's truck. The cop cars were in front of the flatbed, so they were unaware of the plate dropping and Hassan falling out onto the flatbed floor.

Behind the seat in the truck was a cabin space large enough to store just about anything. What Hassan did when he bought the truck was to cut that storage space in half vertically, and separate it with a built in wall. To the naked eye, when and if you were to open the cabin, you wouldn't be able to see or notice what was on the other side of that wall. This was one of the many stash spots he had in his truck, and normally he would transport bricks of cocaine in that compartment.

When the truck flipped over, everything was moving fast, and Hassan's brain kicked into overdrive. At one point he thought about giving up and letting the cops help him out of the truck, but then the small explosion occurred and the fire was starting to enter the truck. The heat made him think fast, because he did not want to be burned alive. He saw that the grille to the storm drain could be moved, and out of nowhere, the movie Swordfish popped into his head. He remembered what John Travolta said about Houdini making an elephant disappear by diverting the people's attention to somewhere else. That's just what he did when he finally freed his leg from underneath the steering wheel. He figured that if the cops saw that the grille was moved, they would think that he went down into the sewer system. This diverted their attention to that instead of the truck itself.

Hassan didn't think that the trick would even work, but he crawled into the stash compartment and rode it out. He opened up the stash spot's exit door just enough to breathe fresh air while the smoke filled the truck. The only thing he couldn't do was stop the hot metal from burning the skin on his back. That little stash spot in the truck was probably the only thing that didn't catch on fire, but it most definitely got hot.

When the firemen flipped the truck over onto its wheels, he busted his mouth on the toolbox that was back there with him. His back was burnt, his leg was broken, and his mouth was busted up, but he was free. All he had to do now was get the hell off of the moving flatbed without being spotted.

Cindy parked her car two blocks away from Bartrum High School where she and Carlos were supposed to meet. The entire way there she couldn't help but to think about what or who she was leaving behind in the event that she didn't make it out alive. Lil' Rodney's voice kept playing in her head: "Mommy! Mommy!" and the look on Drake's face when he stormed out of the room was also hard not to think about.

Cindy walked alongside the schoolyard fence, looking over into the yard to see if anyone was there. She spotted someone sitting on the school steps. It appeared that he was smoking a cigarette, but she wasn't sure. It was dark and quiet, and nothing was moving except for the occasional car driving down the street.

She pulled her cell phone out of her jacket pocket and kept her finger on the trigger of her gun in her other pocket, ready to start shooting at any moment. From the looks of the area, she definitely would have enough time to engage in a nice little shootout before the cops got there.

"Ah, mama! I see you made it," Carlos said when he answered his phone. "For a minute there I didn't think that you were coming."

"Yeah, well I'm here. So, how do you want to do this?" she asked as she gripped the .40-cal in her pocket.

"It's simple. As soon as you set foot in the schoolyard, the game begins. When you feel close enough, just start shooting. The winner gets to go home to his or her family," he said nonchalantly.

"And how do I know you're not setting me up?" Cindy asked, taking a good look around before entering the schoolyard.

"Because there will never be a day that I let a woman be more of a man than I am!" he spat, then hung up his phone.

He then stood and walked down the school steps with an SK assault rifle in his hand. Surprisingly, he stuck to his word and had come alone, bringing only himself and his gun. He felt like he had something to prove in dealing with Cindy. She was only a woman, and no matter how much work she put in on the streets of Philadelphia, it made no difference, he felt she was beneath him.

He walked out into the middle of the schoolyard, in plain sight where Cindy was sure to see him, and she did.

Cindy stood at the entrance to the yard and looked at the vast open space she was walking into. She pulled the .40-cal from her jacket pocket and checked to make sure that there was one in the chamber. She did the same to the other .40-cal that was stuffed in her back pocket as well.

Entering the schoolyard, it reminded her of an old western movie. The wind was blowing, the air was cold, and the only thing that provided any light was the full moon. Carlos was about 40 yards away, and the closer she got, the more her body tensed up.

At 35 yards, Carlos cocked his weapon.

At 30 yards, Cindy began walking faster.

At 25 yards, all hell broke loose. The SK rang out like the sound of a roller coaster in high gear.

Not wanting to be a stationary target, Cindy never ran so fast in her life in an attempt to outrun the barrage of bullets flying in her direction. She shot back over her shoulder as she ran across the yard, which forced Carlos to also move. Unlike Cindy, who packed handguns, his gun was a lot bigger than hers, so it was harder for him to run carrying the extra weight.

For about thirty seconds they looked as though they were playing laser tag, running back and forth, rolling around on the ground and zigzagging throughout the schoolyard, trying to get a good shot off to end this gun battle.

Cindy popped her empty clip out, reached into her jacket pocket and grabbed another one and slammed it into the smoking .40-cal. At the same time, she took the second .40-cal out of her back pocket and began firing both guns simultaneously as she walked slowly towards Carlos in an attempt to even up the score of bullets being fired.

Another minute went by, which seemed like an hour, and nobody was hit; only the school building. But the more they ran around, the closer they got to one another. And the closer they got to one another, the more Carlos could hear the bullets breezing by his head. He let the SK rip one more time before the clip emptied. He tossed it to the ground and pulled out a 17-shot Barretta.

Before he could get a shot off, one of Cindy's bullets struck him in his hip and dropped him to his knee. Seeing this, she zeroed in on him and dropped the gun in her left hand in order to cup the gun in her right hand so that she could fire more accurately at her target. Carlos fired back at her. One bullet just missed her face but took a huge chunk out of her left ear. Another bullet struck her in the chest, causing her to stumble backwards, but not dropping her. The adrenaline in her body was racing so much that the bullet that hit her vest didn't even knock the wind out of her.

Cindy thought about everything that made her angry, like Big Rodney dying, Chris and Rob trying to kill her, and D-Rock raping her. She thought about Lil' Rodney running up to her and screaming, "Mommy! Mommy!" and she thought about the promise that she made to Drake that she would be coming home.

She was only about 20 feet away from Carlos, and the next shot she fired hit him in the shoulder and knocked him to the ground. He fired another shot that hit her in the leg, but she returned with two more, hitting him in his chest and stomach and laid him flat on his back. He wasn't dead yet, but very close to it. The gun he had in his hand became useless as his body began to go into shock from his wounds.

Cindy walked over to him and kicked the gun from his hand. His eyes were wide open and steam was coming from his mouth as he breathed heavily. This was the moment of truth… the very moment that Cindy was waiting for, ever since she found out that Carlos wanted her dead. She squatted over him and watched as he struggled to breathe. She stared into his eyes as he looked up at her.

The sound of a police car snapped her eyes away from his, and she knew that it wouldn't be much longer before they swarmed the area in response to multiple gunshots being fired.

She leaned over and kissed Carlos on his forehead the way the Italians do right before they whack one of their own. She didn't do it because she felt any love or sympathy for him, but rather due to the fact that he had the courage to stand toe to toe in an all-out gun battle with her like a true gangsta would. She stood up, pointed the gun at his head and fired the final shot, taking him out of his suffering. Then she dropped the .40-cal on his chest.

She walked away slowly into the night, leaving behind a burden she no longer had to carry.

"FBI!" Pesco yelled out before kicking in the door to Hassan's last known address where he hadn't lived for years.

Door after door was kicked in throughout South Philly, and just about every other door was knocked on. Whoever answered was questioned about Hassan's whereabouts. Some people were willing to help if they ever came across Hassan, but the people who knew him—which was almost everybody in South Philly—declined the invitation to help capture him under any circumstances… that is until a $20,000 reward for his arrest went out over the news. After that, all kinds of phone calls were coming into the Tip Line with reports of Hassan being in the neighborhood, even though he wasn't.

The one thing about being the most wanted man in the city with a $20,000 reward over your head and only about $5,500 in your pocket was that there weren't too many places you could hide. Hassan went to the only place where no one was even thinking about him; a place where he could relax and get the proper medical treatment for his wounds; a place where he didn't have to worry about the Feds or cops, or people seeking to cash in on his arrest. This was where he could lay around in his boxers all day, and get room service with some of the best home cooked meals a man had ever tasted. Hassan went to a place where he would be loved. He went to his grandmother's house, Ms. Eleanor Knight. She lived in North Philly, and she was unknown to just about everybody. She was his biological father's mother, and only Hassan and his mother knew that she existed.

When Hassan's mother, Wanda, was about three months pregnant with him, his biological father, David, died in a car accident. Hassan's mother was young and running the streets back in those days, and his real dad wasn't the only one that she was sleeping with at that time. When his dad died, she convinced a naïve Muslim brother named Abdullah that he was the father. That's how Hassan got the Muslim name, and that's what he grew up thinking, until Eleanor spotted him and his mother at a hospital one day.

Eleanor remembered Wanda from all the times that David had brought her to the house. The first time she laid eyes on Hassan, she felt something stir within her soul. There he was, at the age of eight, looking just like her son, David. He was the spitting image of David, and not even Wanda could deny it.

Not wanting Hassan to deny his bloodline, Wanda agreed to introduce Ms. Eleanor as a friend of the family, only until Hassan was old enough to understand everything. Plus, she had to figure out how to tell Abdullah that Hassan wasn't his son. But before Wanda had the chance to do that, Abdullah had died.

When Hassan got older, he and Eleanor became very close, and when he found out about the story of his biological father, it brought them even closer together.

One thing for sure is that Hassan felt safe in her hands, and the only thing he needed to do right now was get some rest, and try to figure out a way to get out of the city without being killed or turned in. He thought about calling Cindy, but it was too early. Also, he wasn't sure whether or not her phone was being tapped, and he definitely wasn't willing to find out. For now, it was time to eat; cabbage, macaroni and cheese, candied yams and boneless fried chicken breast.

Drake sat on the edge of the bed as he stared at the television news, waiting to see Cindy's face pop up on the screen. He was pissed, but more concerned about her wellbeing. If given the chance, he would have been standing by her side when facing Carlos, and got the job done for her.

After Cindy left Tracy's house to go meet up with Carlos, Drake waited for a few minutes, then decided to follow her, hoping to give her some assistance in the gun battle. He caught up with her when she got into the city, but Cindy lost him in the midst of the heavy traffic. A near car accident slowed him up enough to watch her fade out of sight. He drove around for a while looking for her, but it was to no avail. All he could do was go back to Tracy's and wait for her to either pop up dead on the 12 o'clock news, or come walking through the door, alive and well.

The headlights flashed through the bedroom window, catching Drake's attention. He looked out of the window to see if it was Cindy, and a huge relief overcame him because it was her. By the way she got out of the car and walked towards the house, she appeared not to have been injured. He jumped back onto the bed and lay down as though he hadn't been waiting up for her. Part of Drake wanted to run and wrap his arms around Cindy but the other part wanted her to know how angry he was for taking a chance with her life, and possibly leaving Lil' Rodney without his mother.

Cindy walked into the bedroom to see Drake lying on the bed with Lil' Rodney asleep next to him. She had a bandage on her ear where Carlos had shot her. She placed the single Glock .40-cal on the dresser and began shedding her clothes, including the bulletproof vest.

Not a word was spoken, and she really didn't want to even look at Drake, because she knew how disappointed he really was. She headed straight to the shower, and it didn't take Drake long to follow her into the bathroom.

"So, what happened?" he asked, leaning against the shower and watching Cindy submerge herself under the hot shower, allowing the blood to freely drip from her ear.

"It's done," she answered, looking into his eyes while under the shower water.

That was another sigh of relief for Drake. He really didn't feel like dealing with the bullshit anymore. He was tired of just about everything, including Cindy's little gangsta antics. All he wanted to do was get as far away from Pennsylvania as possible, find a nice house, and start a family. Being a street runner was getting old, and now all he wanted to do was grow old instead.

"Yo, you had me worried sick," he said as he took off his clothes to join her. "This is it, Cindy. It all ends here and now."

He got into the shower and turned on the second showerhead on the opposite wall. The water beaded off of his back as he wrapped his arms around Cindy and pulled her close to him.

Every time Drake touched her, she could feel her level of security rise. When he held her in his arms, it was as though he never wanted to let her go.

"I love you, Cindy," he said, and turned her around so that she was facing him. "I swear to God, I love you, and I can't afford to lose you," he said as he looked at her wounded ear.

"Drake, you don't have to say anymore. I love you too, baby. And from now on, you don't have to worry about me because I'm done with the streets. It's over. I give you my word," she said, and rested her head against his chest.

She was tired too. And despite the fact that she had a federal warrant, she was willing and ready to give Drake what was left of her mind, body and soul. Tonight, right there in the shower, she was more at peace than she had ever felt in her life. "I'm sorry I lost you earlier," she said, giggling at the thought of dipping and weaving through traffic, knowing that he was following her.

"Yeah, well I'm sorry Mike Tyson got a hold of ya ear!" he joked back, tapping her ear that was missing a little piece of flesh.

She flinched at the stinging sensation and went to bite him on his chest.

They played around in the shower. It was a little fun and a joke for a minute, but the reality of that bullet possibly being two more inches to the left was all too much to continue the laughter.

Drake was just happy that she had made it home. "You know, one day you're going to be my wife."

"Your wife?" Cindy asked, surprised that those words were coming from his mouth.

"Yeah, my wife. And we're going to sit back, relax, and grow old together."

"Well, I think now is a good a time as any to let you know something about me. I hope that you don't look at me differently after I tell you this, but I was going to wait for the right moment," Cindy said, swallowing hard.

Drake didn't know what to think. He took a step back and looked her up and down jokingly, like he was looking for any surgical scars he might have missed. He waited to hear what she had to say.

"Baby, I'm pregnant," Cindy said with a huge smile on her face. "You should see the look on ya face, boo!" she said, laughing at him.

Drake was still processing the words that came out of her mouth. He was speechless at first. This changed everything—for the better, that is, and once again he was going to be a daddy. Words couldn't express the way he felt, so the best thing that he could do was to kiss her, and he did that over and over again. At this moment, Drake felt more blessed than ever. Cindy had given him the greatest gift and this time he would do everything in his power to protect the woman he loved and their unborn child.

Chapter 13

If you left it up to Grandma, Hassan would never have to leave her house, especially since he was her only grandchild. He loved his grandmother to death, but he just had to go outside and get some air for a few minutes while Ms. Eleanor ran her daily errands. She watched the news regularly, so she was well aware that he was on the run from the law. But it didn't matter, because he was her grandbaby. If she caught him outside, she'd probably curse him out for being stupid. That's why he loved her so much.

Hassan's leg was healing nicely after Ms. Eleanor snapped it back into place and splinted it up nice and tight. He walked two blocks to 29th and Lehigh, which took him every bit of fifteen minutes, and when he finally made it to the Chinese store, he didn't even want anything.

He glanced over and saw a pay phone that he desperately wanted to use. He only wanted to call Cindy to see if she was alright, and to let her know that he was okay for now, but it seemed like everybody that walked past him stared at him kind of hard. He thought that someone might notice who he was and try to call the cops on him. Hell, he was paranoid like shit, and even the lady in the Chinese store was looking suspect.

It was a must. He had to call Cindy. He went back into the store, got change for a dollar, and then limped back outside to the pay phone. He hesitated, thinking that the police would be able to track him down from this phone call. Then he thought about making the phone call short so that they wouldn't be able to, just like he had seen many times in the movies. But he quickly realized that shit doesn't work. If they did come, he definitely wouldn't be able to run, and he thought about that too. He stood in front of the phone trippin' out for about five to ten minutes before he just said, "Fuck it!"

Cindy was sitting on the back porch of Tracy's house, watching the kids play around in the snow. The last time that she had heard from Hassan, he was in the middle of being chased by the cops, which was about two weeks ago. Her phone rang, and when she looked down at the screen, it was a number that she didn't recognize. She almost didn't answer it at first, but something inside of her said that it might be Hassan. "Yo, who's dis?" she answered, standing up to go back into the house to get better reception.

"What's good wit' you, baby girl?" Hassan replied, glad to hear a familiar voice once again.

Cindy went nuts when she heard his voice on the other end of the phone. She'd been worried sick about him, and had so much to tell him about everything that had happened since he's been MIA "He-e-e-ey, cousin!" she said with a big smile on her face, overwhelmed with joy.

"Look I don't have long because I don't know if your phone is tapped, and I don't want the police to—"

"No! No! This phone ain't tapped. The only three people who have this number are you, Drake and my lawyer, so you're cool, cousin. Trust me," she said with confidence.

"So, what's been going on? How's Drake and Rodney?"

"They're good. Everybody's good over here, except for the fact that I have a warrant out for my arrest. The Feds want to see me under the jail, but you know I can't go for dat. But fuck all dat! Where the hell are you?" she asked, concerned about his wellbeing.

"I'm down North Philly right now. I'm trying to find a way out of the city before they end up burying me here, ya dig me?"

The last thing Cindy wanted to see was her cousin going to prison for the rest of his life, or even worse, get himself killed by the police who were still on the hunt for him. They've been through so much together, and he was probably all the family that she had left. It would be impossible to leave him behind. "I'm leaving in two days, and you're welcome to come," she offered, hoping that he would take her up on it. "I think that of all the people, you might like where we're going the most."

"Where the hell might that be?"

"Well… I'll tell you when I come to pick you up tomorrow," she said, not really giving him a choice.

Hassan trusted Cindy with his life, so wherever she was planning to go he was with it, as long as it meant getting out of Pennsylvania. "I'll call you tomorrow," he said, then hung up the phone, still a little paranoid about the length of his call.

"Try to relax, we're almost there," the doctor said to Peaches while she took deep breaths, praying for a healthy baby.

She'd been in labor for the past four hours, and due to the umbilical cord being wrapped around the baby's neck, they had to perform an emergency caesarian section. She was hurting, and all she could think about was safely bringing her first and only child into the world. Although Tazz was dead, she was just as happy to have his baby.

The C-section was successful, and Peaches gave birth to a seven pound-three ounce baby girl whom she already had a name for; Alicia. That was Peaches' mother's name.

The doctors left her room so that she could be alone with the baby, especially since she decided to breastfeed. It was her personal time… or so she thought. Moments after the doctors and nurses left, Drake came strolling in with a devious grin on his face. Peaches didn't know what to think. She just sat there, breastfeeding Alicia with a concerned look on her face. The concern became fear once she noticed the handle of a gun poking out from Drake's waist.

"Damn, Peaches, I ain't seen you in a while. Where da hell have you been?" Drake asked, breaking the ice.

"I've been doing okay, Drake. I just got back into the city a few weeks ago. They kicked me out of the program after Villain was killed." She was trying to make small talk because she knew that he was there for a reason. She'd been around Drake long enough to know when he was up to something, and from where she was sitting, she could see it in his eyes. This made her even more afraid for the safety of her and the baby. "How did you know I was here?" she asked, curious because she hadn't seen him since that day in court.

"You know, ever since Villain…" he struggled to say as he thought about Kim and the baby. "You never came around to see how I was doing. You didn't call me or nothing. Not a peep. You just disappeared. So, I tried to look for you, but I couldn't find you, and I thought to myself… You know what? That story is too long. The bottom line is that ya mom called me and told me that you were back in the city, and she thought that I needed to talk to you, seeing that you were pregnant and all. She had this crazy idea that the baby you have in your arms was my baby."

Shit! Peaches thought to herself. She had a long talk with her mom a couple of days after she got back to the city, but she never told her who the baby's father was. She guessed that her mom probably thought that it was Drake's, seeing as he was the only man that she had ever brought home to introduce to her family. Mom was wrong, big time! And now it's possible that it may cost her life once Drake finds out whose baby it is.

"That day you called my phone and told me that Villain knew what was going on, did you tell Villain where I was?" Drake asked, taking a seat in one of the visitor's chairs.

Peaches knew he was there for something, and now it was all starting to come out. *Did he come for revenge because of what Villain had done to his family? Did he come here to shoot me and my child because I was the one who told Villain that Drake was at the hospital with his girlfriend?* These were just a couple of the questions that ran through her head. She knew that the next question Drake was going to ask would be concerning the baby.

"Please don't do this, Drake!" Peaches pleaded, not really wanting to give him an answer. "Drake, I was scared. He was going to kill me if I didn't say anything. I swear, I didn't know that he was going to do what he did," she said, now beginning to cry.

Her answer made Drake furious inside, but he didn't show it. He wanted to kill her for that reason alone. But the reality of the situation, plus knowing what she had gone through before giving Villain that piece of information, brought him to accept the fact that most women were weak. The blame should only fall on him for putting her in a situation where she had to choose between her life and his. It didn't make it wrong, but it damn sure didn't make it right either.

"Whose baby is that?" he asked, zooming in on the infant sucking on her right nipple.

"It's yours."

"You're lying!"

"Please, Drake! I'm begging you not to do this!" she continued to plead, thinking that if he found out that the baby was Tazz's he would kill it.

"Whose fucking baby is it!" Drake shouted, accidentally getting the attention of a nurse walking past the room.

"Is everything alright in here?" the nurse asked, stopping in the doorway.

"Yeah, everything's good," Drake replied, dismissing the nurse just as quickly as he caught her attention.

After the nurse left with an attitude, Drake walked up to Peaches and looked down at the infant she held against her breast. Even at this early age the baby looked just like Tazz.

Peaches looked up at Drake with fear in her eyes. It was the same kind of fear that Kim had in her eyes right before Villain shot her. If Drake wanted to do something to her, the look on her face alone would have stopped him. But he didn't come to the hospital to hurt her. His only reason for being there was to see if the rumor about the baby being his was true. Peaches did all that crying and pleading for nothing. It must have been her guilty conscious messing with her.

"You take care of yourself," he leaned over and whispered in her ear before turning away and exiting the room.

Peaches let out a sigh of relief as the tears continued to flow from her eyes. She knew that this would probably be the last time she'd ever see Drake again, and despite the fact that she thought that he was there to kill her, a part of her still loved him.

Betrayal is the ultimate sign of disrespect. It can't be forgiven, not even if the person who was betrayed tries to forgive you. This was something that Peaches would have to live with forever, and every time she looked at Alicia, she would be reminded of how disloyal she was. It may not matter now, but when Alicia got older, it would be difficult for Peaches to explain how she had conceived her.

As for Drake, this was another closed chapter in his book. It was nothing for him to dwell on, nothing to regret, just motivation to move forward with his life.

Tracy and Cindy sat at the kitchen table going over the place and location of where Tracy's ranch house was. It wasn't being used, so it would be a perfect getaway home where Cindy could raise her family without being bothered by the locals. Being all the way on the other side of the United States was the ideal way of ducking the Feds. The last place they would look for Cindy is Seattle, Washington, and before the day was over, she and Rodney would receive new identifications. Hassan already had a fake driver's license, birth certificate and Social Security card, so he was straight.

"I've got a surprise for you," Tracy said, shuffling through a folder full of paperwork. She pulled a deed to eight acres of land from the folder that the four-bedroom, four and a half bathroom ranch sat on. It had a small horse stable and a large barn, both without the animals. Tracy bought the land for a cheap price from one of her clients who was going to declare bankruptcy. She thought it would be good for her when she had to make business trips to the West Coast, but as it turned out, most of the time she just stayed at a hotel. "I'm giving you and Drake this house as a gift," she said, passing Cindy the deed. "Now, for the moment I'm going to put it in Derrick's name until you're clear of your warrants. If you don't like it after about seven years, then it's okay for you to sell it. I don't want anything from it. But for now, this is my early wedding gift to you two," she said with a smile.

All Cindy could do was thank her. This was a gift that would never be forgotten, and one that was well appreciated. She didn't have any plans on living the fast life anymore, so this was just what she needed. This was a place where she could fall all the way back and live the slow, country life that she often dreamed about. And hearing Tracy say something about a wedding brought a smile to her face, and only she knew the reason behind it. Marriage was never in her plans, but it damn sure didn't sound that bad when she thought about it, especially having someone like Drake for a husband.

Thinking about him, Drake came walking through the door like clockwork. Cindy and Tracy were just about to go over the flight arrangements for tomorrow. Because he was doing a lot of last minute running around and they didn't want to be late, they had to inform him of exactly what time they were leaving.

Drake walked over to the refrigerator to grab something to drink, when a shadow running past the kitchen window caught his attention. For a second he thought it was one of the kids, but the sound of screeching tires in front of the house easily changed that thought.

Cindy and Tracy both got up from the table to look out of the window. Once Cindy saw the letters "FBI" on the back of one of the agent's jackets, she just put her head down and thought that all of her plans to leave Philly were going down the drain. Tracy walked to the front of the house to get a better view of how many law enforcement officers were outside, and there were plenty.

Agent Pesco led the charge, and before kicking the door down he called Tracy's home phone in hopes that he could get Cindy to surrender without using violence. He wanted to avoid any casualties on both sides.

Drake came from the back of the house with a 12-gauge pump strapped to his back, two 17-shot 9-mm Barrettas, and a bulletproof vest he stopped in the living room to put on. The plane tickets were in his back pocket. There was no doubt that he was ready to go to war with the Feds, but he just wasn't thinking clearly. His intentions were good, but not really that smart. He was acting on his emotions instead of dealing with logic. For Cindy, he was willing to ride or die.

But the reality of the situation was that he was more likely to die going up against the very large number of federal agents surrounding the house with guns that Drake never knew existed. It would be a loss all across the board, and Cindy could see this with her own eyes.

"Hey! Don't be stupid, Derrick!" Tracy yelled, and darted across the room to stop Drake from going out the front door. "You're committing suicide! Boy, are you crazy?"

"I can't let 'em take her!" he said, clutching the Barettas tightly in his hands.

"We've got kids in the house!" Tracy pleaded, hoping that would be enough to calm him down.

Cindy walked over to Drake. Her head was down so he couldn't see the hurt in her eyes. She stopped in front of him and slowly put her hands on the two 9-mms. She looked up at him, and it was at that point he could see the hurt and pain that she was feeling. He could also see the disapproval of doing what he was about to do. Seeing this, he slowly let the guns go into her hands, and she passed them to Tracy.

"You're gonna be a great daddy," Cindy said, putting one of his hands on her stomach. "I'ma fight this in the courts. And if that don't work, you can always come bust me out of jail," she said jokingly, but crying at the same time.

This was the second worst feeling that Drake ever felt; the first one being the loss of Kim and the baby; and now, the feeling of losing Cindy and his unborn baby. This was the first time he shed a tear for anything in a long time. His feelings for Cindy were clear, and the fact that he was restricted from doing anything to help her made it difficult to hold them back.

The house phone continued to ring. Tracy got tired of it and picked it up. "Hello," she said, putting the phone on speaker so that everyone could hear.

"This is Agent Pesco of the FBI, and I'm only calling as a courtesy for the two children you have inside the home. All I want is for Cindy to step outside, alone and unarmed. Complying will avoid a lot of unnecessary drama," he announced over the phone.

Cindy walked over to the phone, took it off speaker and picked up the receiver. Turning herself in was probably the hardest thing she ever had to do. She knew exactly how much time she was facing, and the chances of her winning at trial with a bunch of people ratting on her were one in a million. "Just give me about 10 minutes to say goodbye to my son, then I'll come outside. Can I do that much?" she asked.

"Don't do anything stupid, Cindy. The place is surrounded and you're very much considered armed and dangerous," Pesco said, warning her that he and his men will fire upon any threat. "I'm not supposed to do this, but I'm going to give you 10 minutes to say your goodbyes. After that, I've gotta come in and get you," he said, then hung up the phone.

Cindy turned around and walked towards the stairs,

trying her best to figure out a way to say goodbye to Lil' Rodney. How could she tell him that she failed as a mother? How could she explain to this little boy that she was going away for a long time, and she wouldn't be around to see him ride a bike for the first time, or take him to school on his first day? How could she tell him that she wouldn't be able to throw him birthday parties, or take him trick or treating on Halloween? No graduation, no Christmas Day dinners, no football games, no basketball games, no talking to him about the birds and the bees…

All this broke her down as she tried to make it up the steps. She just wanted to say goodbye, go back down the stairs and walk right out of the front door without saying a word. Tracy found it hard to control her emotions, because she cried as though it was her walking up those steps.

As soon as Cindy got upstairs, Lil' Rodney came running out of the bedroom and into her arms. She picked him up, took him to the bedroom and they sat down on the bed. This was harder than she thought it was going to be. It would be impossible for Cindy to tell her son she was going away.

"Mommy, what's wrong?" Lil' Rodney asked, fumbling with a toy robot in his hands.

Somehow, kids always know when something is wrong, no matter how innocent they are. Cindy was hurting inside, but she knew that she had to pull it together for the sake of her son.

"Mommy is on her way to the store, and I was wondering if you wanted anything while I was out," she said, already regretting lying to him about where she was going.

"No, Mommy. I don't want anything. Just hurry back so we can say our ABCs together," he responded, burning a hole right through her heart.

"Okay," she said, kissing him on the forehead before leaving. She couldn't sit there any longer. She walked back downstairs and basically melted into Tracy's arms, now crying uncontrollably.

Drake just stood off to the side, seeing that this was a mother-to-mother connection and had nothing to do with him.

"He's going to be well taken care of, I promise you that. And if I've got to bring him to see you every week myself, then that's what I'm willing to do," Tracy said, comforting Cindy the best way she knew how.

This was something that Cindy needed. Doing time, whether it's in the penitentiary or during pretrial, can be difficult if you don't have the right support system on the outside to help you through those rough days. Tracy had only known Cindy for about a month, but the time they spent together grew into a meaningful friendship; better than other friendships that had lasted for years. In fact, Tracy was probably the only female friend Cindy ever had, and she pretty much trusted every word that came out of her mouth.

Cindy walked over to Drake, who was sitting on the couch with the saddest look on his face. It made her smile just a little, seeing his puppy dog face. She tried to find the right words to say, but she couldn't. She just sat on his lap, wrapped her arms around him and kissed his lips softly.

Drake wasn't up for the sad goodbye shit, so his words were simple and straight to the point. His mind was already made up, and there was nothing anybody could do to change it. "I'll come and see you soon," he said, kissed her, and then tapped her on the butt, motioning for her to get up.

The house phone rang again, and everyone knew that it was Agent Pesco calling to let Cindy know that her 10 minutes were up.

Cindy picked up the phone. "I'm on my way out," she said, then hung up. She flipped open her cell phone and called Brian McMonigal, her lawyer, as she walked to the front door.

Drake walked her outside, where she was met by Agent Pesco. "I love you, babe!" he said, and kissed her for the last time. "Don't forget what I said, you hear me?"

She nodded her head, still holding her cell phone to her ear. Pesco called a female agent over to search Cindy before they put her in the car. By then, Brian had answered the phone. "Cindy, what can I do for you?"

"The Feds are arresting me now. I'll see you downtown in a couple of hours. I guess it's your turn to start fighting," she said, and hung up the phone and turned it over to the Feds so that she could be handcuffed.

Agent Pesco stared at Drake, and Drake couldn't help but to notice it. It made Drake a little uncomfortable. It was as if Pesco was thinking about arresting him too. He remembered that Brian had said that there were no warrants on him, and the only person who could get him locked up was Tazz. But Tazz was dead, and that gave Drake a little extra boost of confidence to be arrogant. "What the fuck are you staring at me for?" Drake asked aggressively as he stared right back at Pesco.

"I just wanted to get a good look at the infamous Drake. If you don't get your life together, I'll be coming for you next," Pesco warned.

"Well, I got a good look at you too, so if I see you coming for me—"

"Drake!" Cindy yelled from the back seat of the agent's car, cutting him off before he ended up threatening a federal agent. She shook her head no, basically telling him to shut up. He did so, even though he wanted to say more. He just gave Pesco a smile, then turned around and walked back into the house.

Chapter 14

"All rise!" the bailiff announced when the Honorable Judge Watson entered the courtroom.

"Good morning. This is the matter of the United States versus Cynthia McParsons. Would counsel state their names for the record?" Judge Watson asked, looking down at the complaint and warrant.

Cindy sat at the defendant's table with Brian, hoping to get bail so that she could fight her case from the streets. Tracy and Drake sat in the back of the courtroom, ready and willing to put up anything if bail was set.

Brian was going to do all he could to see to it that Cindy could at least be put on house arrest until trial.

"Do both counsel agree to a bail in this matter?" the judge asked, already knowing that the government would deny bail.

"Your Honor, Ms. McParsons is not a flight risk, and we have her family in back of the courtroom right now, willing to help out with any bail. Also, Your Honor, I have written statements from people in the neighborhood where Ms. McParsons grew up, stating how she's been an asset to the neighborhood. We also have over five hundred signatures from the recreation centers in South Philadelphia who will vouch for her release. It is because of Ms. McParsons that there are clean playgrounds for children to play. And because of her contribution to the community, there are fewer drugs being sold on the street corners, and families are provided sufficient housing through the Section 8 program. Your Honor, I think it would be more of a benefit to allow her to fight these drug allegations from home where she can also tend to her four-year old child and get proper prenatal care because she's two months pregnant."

"You speak of Ms. McParsons as though she's a saint," the judge said, impressed with McMonigal's speech. "If I were to hear just your side, Ms. McParsons would probably be released on her own recognizance. But I'm quite sure that the government has a rebuttal to this."

"Yes, Your Honor, I have plenty to say," the prosecutor, Mr. Williams, stated in rebuttal. "Your Honor, Ms. McParsons—or Cindy, which is what the people in the streets call her—is far from a saint. This woman is one of the most notorious drug dealers to come out of the City of Philadelphia. The government has substantial evidence of her selling over one hundred bricks of cocaine in South Philadelphia and elsewhere, some of which was manufactured into crack by the defendant. We have several witnesses who will testify to her making a call to kill one of her competitors in the drug game. We also have another witness who will testify to being shot by her in a project hallway. That shooting was a direct connection to her killing the victim's closest friend, Christopher Hopkins, less than a year ago."

"We have also launched a separate investigation on Ms. McParsons possibly killing her supplier, Mr. Carlos Hector Gonzales. As soon as the DNA report comes back on the blood found at the scene, we will know more."

"The bottom line, Judge, is that Ms. McParsons is more than just a flight risk. She has the potential to kill again if you let her back on the streets. She has access to plenty of drug money, and the government believes that if this Honorable Court releases her, we may never see her again. And, I'm not even mentioning the fact that she is the head of a drug empire that grosses an average of eight-million dollars a year."

"Okay. Okay, I understand," the judge said, hearing more than enough. "How many people are on the indictment?" he asked the prosecutor, taking his glasses off and placing them on the bench.

"Your Honor, we have a 29-man indictment, with Cindy taking the leadership role," the prosecutor responded.

"How many will be testifying so far?" the judge wanted to know. He knew that somebody had to be snitching.

"Eighteen are cooperating thus far, and we believe that number will rise before trial."

Cindy sat in her chair and almost had a heart attack. Based on the picture the prosecutor had painted of her, she would keep her ass locked up too. She initially believed her attorney did very well and there was a significant chance of her getting bail, but after the prosecutors ripped her to shreds, Cindy knew that chance was zilch. As expected, the judge denied bail without even going into recess to give it consideration. He remanded her to the custody of U.S. Marshals, and she was to be held until trial.

Brian quickly asked the judge for a speedy trial. He was already seasoned in dealing with rats, and by the looks of things, that's mostly what he would be dealing with. There was no physical evidence against Cindy, because most of the time when she did deal drugs, she used the pen and pad technique, so the wiretaps wouldn't be helpful at all.

Cindy looked to the back of the courtroom where Drake and Tracy were sitting. She had a disgusted look on her face, mainly because her bail was denied, and she actually thought that she might have a chance. *Drake looks so good*, she thought to herself as the marshal came over to her table to take her back down to the holding area.

"We love you, Cindy!" Tracy yelled out from the back of the courtroom when Cindy stood up.

"Keep ya head up, babe!" Drake yelled out, wanting Cindy to stay stress free so that she wouldn't end up having a miscarriage. "I'll see you tomorrow on the visit!" he reminded her.

Drake hated to see her like this. He had made big plans for the both of them, and now he was watching those plans go down the drain, especially since the bail attempt went south. He knew that he had to do something, and he had to do it quickly. Trial was in six months, and just about everyone who was cooperating with the government was already in custody, so it would be impossible to get to them.

He thought about trying to pay everybody off not to testify against Cindy, but even if he offered that, there were still at least five or six people out of the 18 who were facing a life sentence. So, if they were snitching, it was to save their own lives, and there would be no amount of money that could keep a rat from trying to save his own tail.

Court was pretty rough yesterday, and all Cindy thought about was getting to see Drake and Lil' Rodney on the visit. As soon as she walked onto the visiting room floor, Lil' Rodney ran over to her, happy to see his mommy for the first time in a few weeks.

When Drake stood up to kiss her, he stuffed a small balloon into her mouth, and without question, she immediately swallowed it. "Throw it up as soon as you get upstairs, and hold onto it until the time is right," he whispered in her ear and gave her a sinister look. "You look beautiful," he said softly, pinching her chin before sitting down. "Ya face is getting full too. You got that baby glow."

Cindy smiled as she picked Rodney up and sat him on her lap. She missed him so much. The reality of her situation started to kick in, and there were times when she even thought about killing herself, but she couldn't bring herself to do it. Looking around the visiting room, this was not the way she wanted to spend possibly the rest of her life, and the smile she gave to Drake was only to cover up the pain she felt.

"They gave me a trial date for July 20th," she said, looking down at her son while he drank his juice. "Brian said that he was ready, but I don't think he really is. There's just too much evidence to look through."

"Hey, look at me. What did I tell you before you turned yourself over to the Feds? I said that I've got you, babe."

"Yeah, but—"

"Stop, Cindy! There are no buts. You just got to have faith in me. Just trust me."

"Faith! Faith!" Cindy snapped back. "I'm in a secure federal facility, and every time I go to court I'm shackled and transported underground to where I can't even see the outside! I sit around all day doing nothing, thinking about all the rat muthafuckas tellin' on me after I done took care of them better than anyone else! I'm facing the rest of my life in prison, and all you can say is, 'Have faith in me'! I'm sorry if I don't have any faith right now. As far as I'm concerned, faith is part of the reason why I'm sitting here now. My fuckin' baby might be born in a jail cell, and as soon as I have it, the people are just going to take it away. And you want me to have faith? Fuck faith, Drake!"

She was letting him have it, not because she was angry at him, but more so mad at herself for putting herself in this predicament. She was just letting out her frustrations, and the only person that she could do that with was the man she loved.

Drake understood fully. That's why he didn't take anything she said to heart. In fact, he just sat there and chuckled at her, listening to her talk like this for the first time. It sounded kinda cute to him. "Are you done?" he asked as he sat back in his chair with a smile on his face. "You know, one day you're going to learn how to trust me."

"And what's that supposed to mean?" she shot back at him with an attitude.

"Nothing. Just enjoy the rest of the visit with your son," he said, waving her off as though he was finished talking, and turned his smile into a quick frown.

What am I doing? she asked herself. Why am I snapping at Drake like this? All this man has ever done was stick by my side through the good and the bad, and here I go, talking to him like he's to blame for me being in jail. She just sat there in silence.

For the rest of the visit, they both sat in silence, except for when Cindy talked to Lil' Rodney. She didn't even know how to apologize to Drake for snapping at him, or if he was even willing to accept her apology. All she could do was enjoy the couple of hours she had left of her visit with her son. She loved Drake for sure, but she also had a lot of pressure on her and she only hoped Drake understood that.

Chapter 15

SIX MONTHS LATER, THE DAY BEFORE TRIAL

Cindy sat on the edge of her bunk, rubbing her belly. Her stomach was as big as a house, and the continuous kicking from the baby kept her from falling asleep. Cindy waddled over to her locker and took out the letter from Drake that she had gotten earlier that day, but didn't read yet. It had been a few days since she'd spoken to him over the telephone, and as of late the visits slowed up, which made her feel like he was moving on. It was the day before she went to pick her jury, and this was probably the loneliest she had ever felt. Not even Tracy took the time out to come see her.

She took the letter out of the envelope and read it:

Cindy finished reading the letter and just stared at the wall, thinking about what she just read. "The time is right," she mumbled to herself, pondering what Drake meant.

Then, a lightbulb went off in her head and she remembered the balloon that he had given her on his first visit. She looked over at her celly that was caught up reading her own letter and not paying Cindy any attention. Cindy grabbed the container of baby powder she kept the balloon in and dumped everything out on the table. She blew the powder off of the balloon once she found it.

Cindy took a razor and gently cut the balloon. In it were two pills and a little note that read, "*Take me*", with a smiley face on it. *What the fuck is this?* she wondered as she looked at the pills. All she could think about was Drake's voice saying, "*Trust me*".

She sat back on her bunk, debating whether or not to take the medication. She said, "Fuck it!" and threw both of the pills into her mouth and swallowed them without drinking any water. She waited for something to happen. The entire time she sat there, she thought about whether or not the pills she just took would affect the baby, and for a minute she regretted taking them.

Three minutes went past, and still nothing was happening. She figured that Drake probably gave her some sort of vitamins. She knew that he wouldn't do anything to hurt her or the baby.

She walked over to the desk to clean up the baby powder, and before she could scoop any of it back into the container she felt a funny sensation in her stomach.

It felt like she was pissing on herself, but then it happened. Her water broke, and the fluid splashed onto the floor and caused her celly to jump up.

"Shit, girl! You're going into labor!" her celly said, and pushed the panic button by the door.

Now Cindy was really wondering what Drake had given her. She wasn't due to have the baby until next month, and here she was, feeling contractions that hurt like hell.

The guard came to the door and saw Cindy holding the bottom of her stomach. Her celly didn't hesitate to yell at him, telling the stupid guard that Cindy was going into labor.

It was about 11:30 p.m., so most of the medical staff had gone for the day. The nurse who was on duty came to the cell immediately, but not before setting up a transport unit to take Cindy to the nearest hospital, which was Jefferson Hospital, a mere five or six blocks away.

The contractions were coming on fast, so they had to get her out of there quickly or else she and the baby could be in danger. They put her on a stretcher and wheeled her out of the unit.

The other female inmates were standing at their cell doors watching everything unfold. Most of them liked Cindy, so they stood at their doors and encouraged her to be strong.

"Please don't let me have my baby in this jail!" Cindy begged the nurse, who was pushing the stretcher.

"Don't worry. We're going to get you to the hospital, Ms. McParsons," she responded, trying to make Cindy feel better.

Before Cindy looked up, she was being put in an ambulance. She was escorted by four armed correctional officers; two rode in the ambulance with her, one followed the ambulance in an institution van, and another followed the van in an institution car.

They pulled into the hospital emergency room where it was very crowded, but nurses were on deck, taking her into one of the delivery rooms. As they transported her into her designated room, she noticed the face of a pregnant woman standing by the pay phones. Cindy couldn't remember where she knew the girl from, and the dark glasses she had on made it even harder to recognize her, so she thought nothing of it.

Two guards stood outside of the room while another sat inside with Cindy as she was delivering the baby. A fourth guard sat outside in the car, keeping an eye on the perimeter of the hospital. Each guard carried the standard 9-mm Barretta with two extra magazines, and wore a bulletproof vest. When civilians saw this, they stared in astonishment.

Cindy's delivery went rather quickly, only taking a few hours, and through blood, screaming, and tears, she delivered a six pound-seven ounce baby girl. She named her Jasmine Alea Henson, and despite the baby coming a month earlier than planned, she was pretty much healthy. Although she was handcuffed to the bed, the obstetrician allowed Cindy to hold the baby before they put her into an incubator.

"We're going to have to transport Ms. McParsons upstairs in a few minutes to the Mother/Baby Wing so that we can get her cleaned up, run a few tests and monitor her condition before we release her," the doctor told the guards sitting in the room.

One of the guards had to step out to make a phone call to the jail's nurse to let her know that Cindy had successfully delivered her baby.

It was bittersweet for Cindy. She was holding her beautiful baby girl in her arms who looked just like her. But the bitter taste of having to leave the hospital without her set in hard. It even made her cry just thinking about it.

It seemed like everything in the emergency room went into slow motion when Amber, the girl with the familiar face, left the pay phones and threw the pillow she had under her shirt that made her look pregnant, onto the floor. She then walked two doors down from Cindy's room and tapped on the glass door, motioning Hassan to fall in behind her. He did so swiftly and on point, taking the safety off of his .45 automatic.

The one guard sat in a chair facing Cindy, and the other one stood at the door, looking in the opposite direction from where Amber and Hassan were coming from. Amber passed by him first, catching his attention, and by the time he saw Hassan, it was too late. The muffled sounds of the bullets passing through the silencer gave the guard an initial shock before they entered his side at close range and sent excruciating pain throughout his entire body. Before the second guard got a chance to stand up, Hassan put the gun to the back of his head.

Cindy, who was still handcuffed to the bed, knew exactly what Hassan was about to do, so she turned over and shielded the baby in order to avoid her getting hit by a stray bullet in case it exited through the guard's head. Hassan pulled the trigger, and the only thing that came out of the guard's head was blood.

The silencer muffled the sounds of the shots, but the flash from the gun was bright enough to get the attention of the medical staff in the emergency room, and everyone there went into a panic.

Amber entered the room and began searching through the pockets of the guard lying on the ground and holding his side. She disarmed him, and then found the key to the handcuffs. "I got it!" she yelled out to Hassan, who was watching the door for the other guard.

Amber ran over and uncuffed Cindy, who got right up, took the blanket off of the bed, wrapped the baby in it, and tied it over one shoulder like a sling.

Amber passed her the guard's gun as they headed towards the exit. Instead of going right out the front door, they took the back way, running through the hospital hallways until they reached the cafeteria.

The third guard ran back into the emergency room after seeing everyone running out and screaming at the top of their lungs. He pulled his firearm out as he walked up to the room Cindy was in, and the first thing that took him by surprise was a fellow officer sitting in a chair with his brains blown out. The guard on the floor pointed to the back door that Cindy ran out of, and managed to say, "They... they ran through there... McParsons... a male and another female..."

Hassan fired several bullets through the kitchen window that shattered the glass and kicked it out of the frame. The cafeteria was on the ground level at the side of the hospital, and the jump to the pavement was less than five feet, which nobody had a problem with.

Nickie sat in a dark tinted minivan right below the window, watching out of the rearview mirror as everyone got into the van. She pulled off down the back streets at a normal speed, trying her best not to draw any attention to herself.

Flashing police car lights were everywhere, but they were all heading towards the emergency room entrance of the hospital.

Nickie shot down 6th Street towards the Benjamin Franklin Bridge. It was so quiet in the van that the only thing you could hear was the engine. Nobody wanted to say a word until they were clear of all the cop cars still heading in the direction of the hospital.

"Welcome home, cousin!" Hassan said, breaking the silence. He leaned over and nudged her in the back seat.

The two pills Drake had given Cindy were to help induce her labor, and he knew that she would have to be taken to the nearest hospital in the area. Since Thomas Jefferson was only a few blocks away from the jail, he came up with a perfect exit strategy.

After witnessing Rick's murder in the Chinese store on 23rd Street and hearing about all the 'hood niggas that were snitching on Cindy, Amber and Nickie were asked by Hassan to help break Cindy out.

The baby began crying for the first time since being born, and Cindy already knew what was wrong with her. She was hungry so she gave her the only milk she could find, which was in her breasts.

Hassan pulled out his cell phone while looking out of the window at the signs going over the bridge.

"What's up, bro?" Drake asked, answering the phone after seeing that it was Hassan calling.

"We got her!" Hassan announced, cutting his eyes over at Cindy as she breastfed the baby. He then passed her the phone.

"Hey, baby!" she said in a low voice so as not to startle the baby.

"Hey, beautiful! How're my girls?"

"We're good!" Cindy said beaming, unable to stop staring at Jasmine.

"Alright. I don't wanna stay on this phone for too long. You should be here in a couple of hours, and I'll see you then."

"Okay, see you soon," she said, and hung up the phone.

Agent Pesco was woken out of his sleep by the sound of his phone ringing. He knew that if anyone was calling him at this time of night, chances are that it wasn't going to be good news. It was Lavinski calling to let him know that Cindy had escaped from the hospital.

Pesco jumped out of bed and got dressed as fast as he could, while Lavinski stayed on the line, giving him the details. When Pesco finally got downstairs and walked out of his front door, Agent Lavinski was sitting on his front steps. He appeared unenthusiastic about trying to apprehend Cindy.

"I've got the video feed from the hospital surveillance. It looks like our friend, Hassan, never left the city," Lavinski said, passing Pesco his cell phone so that he could view the footage.

"Got-damn it!" Pesco snapped. He sat down on the steps in disgust. "You think they'll be stupid enough to stick around?" he asked, looking for a small ray of hope from Lavinski.

"Would you?" he shot back, getting up from the steps and walking towards his car. "Let's go try and find her anyway. That is our job, right?" he said, opening the driver's side door.

Pesco was burning up inside. Cindy sold drugs, killed people, and put the fear of God into just about the entire city. He had her by the balls. It was a concrete case, a guaranteed conviction with a life sentence, and all he had to do was get her in front of a jury. The only thing he forgot—and he sure as hell figured it out by now—is that Cindy didn't have any balls, she had a pussy, and sometimes pussy can make a nigga do some crazy shit. Just ask Drake.

It took Nickie about two and a half hours to get to New York, and during the entire ride Cindy pinched herself several times to see if she was dreaming. It was hard to believe that she was free. Everything had happened so fast. Without question, she was probably the most wanted fugitive on the East Coast. But right now, at this moment going across the Brooklyn Bridge, uncuffed and surrounded by friends and family, she was as free as a bird.

They pulled into the docks behind the Federal Detention Center, MDC Brookline, and the first thing that was noticeable was a huge boat. This was probably the largest ship Cindy or anyone else in the van had ever seen in person.

A large black SUV sat on the dock next to the boat, and getting out of the driver's side was Drake. The warm night breeze lifted his cream colored linen shirt into the air and exposed the white wifebeater underneath it. The headlights from the SUV shone on him as he walked towards the minivan. To Cindy he looked like a superhero. He was. He was her superhero, coming in to sweep her off of her feet.

Amber opened the side door so that Cindy could get out of the van, and when she did, Drake was there to embrace her and the baby with a hug that felt like he never wanted to let her go.

Cindy, for the first time, cried out of joy. Drake looked down at his baby girl, and he too cried out of joy. "I put this on everything, as long as you live, you better never doubt me again!" he said, and pressed his lips against Cindy's for the kiss his heart achingly waited for.

Tracy came walking down the ramp of the boat. She too was happy to see Cindy, but was pressed for time. "We're pulling off in five minutes, so if you're coming, you need to get onboard now or you'll be left out here!" she yelled out, with Lil' Rodney and Lil' Ryan standing next to her.

This was a one-way trip. Whoever was leaving would probably never set foot on United States soil again.

During the past six months, not only was Drake planning Cindy's escape, but he was also establishing a new home in Australia. With a clear record and no warrants, he was able to become the CEO of a small company Tracy owned in that country. They would be living in a small city named Brisbane where Drake had a house built from the ground up, complete with a guest house for Hassan to live in. The house was built deep in the country. The nearest neighbor was two miles away, and the closest town to shop in was about ten miles away. This was every bit of the country life that he and Cindy had talked about.

Hassan wasted no time unloading the SUV, and taking the baby items that Drake had packed for the boat.

Drake walked over to Amber and Nickie and passed them 100-K each for helping Hassan out.

Instead of getting back in the car with Nickie, Amber had other plans, and from the way Hassan hesitated to get on the boat, it seemed as though he felt the same way.

For the past few months, he and Amber had gotten closer. He spent extra time with her while going over the plans to break Cindy out. One thing led to another and the next thing he knew he was laying pipe into her in his grandmother's living room. Hassan definitely wasn't about to miss out on the opportunity to have a constant companion especially during the long ass boat ride to the other side of the world. Besides, Amber was by far one of the baddest 'hood chicks in the city, and with a little bit of molding in the right areas, she could be wifey material. Amber didn't want to miss out on the opportunity to be with him, so she said her goodbyes to her best friend, Nickie, and then walked up the ramp and onto the ship.

Hassan was looking forward to a fresh start. He was leaving Philly behind and had no worries, especially about money, because he too had a little put up for a rainy day. Even though he wasn't going to need it because he'd be working with Drake.

Within minutes, the huge boat left the dock, and no one, not even Nickie, knew where it was going—that is except for the crewmembers and the three new families that became one.

Nickie looked at the boat as it drifted away, and thought about what she was going to do with the money she had. Inspired by Cindy and driven by the way she had South Philly on lock, Nickie headed back to the 'hood with dreams of being a dope girl.

It was true what the old heads say about the streets...

"The game will never change... only the players will."

The End

A KING PRODUCTION

Rich or Famous

Rich Because You Can Buy Fame

A NOVEL

JOY DEJA KING

Welcome To My World

Before I die, if you don't remember anything else I ever taught you, know this. A man will be judged, not on what he has but how much of it. So you find a way to make money and when you think you've made enough, make some more, because you'll need it to survive in this cruel world. Money will be the only thing to save you. As I sat across from Darnell those words my father said to me on his deathbed played in my head.

"Yo, Lorenzo, are you listening to me, did you hear anything I said?"

"I heard everything you said. The problem for you is I don't give a fuck." I responded, giving a casual shoulder shrug as I rested my thumb under my chin with my index finger above my mouth.

"What you mean, you don't give a fuck? We been doing business for over three years now and that's the best you got for me?"

"Here's the thing, Darnell, I got informants all over these streets. As a matter of fact that broad you've had in your back pocket for the last few weeks is one of them."

"I don't understand what you saying," Darnell said swallowing hard. He tried to keep the tone of his voice calm, but his body composure was speaking something different.

"Alexus, has earned every dollar I've paid her to fuck wit' yo' blood suckin' ass. You a fake fuck wit' no fangs. You wanna play wit' my 100 g's like you at the casino. That's a real dummy move, Darnell." I could see the sweat beads gathering, resting in the creases of Darnell's forehead.

"Lorenzo, man, I don't know what that bitch told you but none of it is true! I swear 'bout four niggas ran up in my crib last night and took all my shit. Now that I think about it, that trifling ho Alexus probably had me set up! She fucked us both over!"

I shook my head for a few seconds not believing this muthafucker was saying that shit with a straight face. "I thought you said it was two niggas that ran up in your crib now that shit done doubled. Next thing you gon' spit is that all of Marcy projects was in on the stickup."

"Man, I can get your money. I can have it to

you first thing tomorrow. I swear!"

"The thing is I need my money right now." I casually stood up from my seat and walked towards Darnell who now looked like he had been dipped in water. Watching him fall apart in front of my eyes made up for the fact that I would never get back a dime of the money he owed me.

"Zo, you so paid, this shit ain't gon' even faze you. All I'm asking for is less than twenty-four hours. You can at least give me that," Darnell pleaded.

"See, that's your first mistake, counting my pockets. My money is *my* money, so yes this shit do faze me."

"I didn't mean it like that. I wasn't tryna disrespect you. By this time tomorrow you will have your money and we can put this shit behind us." Darnell's eyes darted around in every direction instead of looking directly at me. A good liar, he was not.

"Since you were robbed of the money you owe me and the rest of my drugs, how you gon' get me my dough? I mean the way you tell it, they didn't leave you wit' nothin' but yo' dirty draws."

"I'll work it out. Don't even stress yourself, I got you, man."

"What you saying is that the nigga you so called aligned yourself with, by using my money and my product, is going to hand it back over to you?"

"Zo, what you talking 'bout? I ain't aligned

myself wit' nobody. That slaw ass bitch Alexus feeding you lies."

"No, that's you feeding me lies. Why don't you admit you no longer wanted to work for me? You felt you was big shit and could be your own boss. So you used my money and product to buy your way in with this other nigga to step in my territory. But you ain't no boss you a poser. And your need to perpetrate a fraud is going to cost you your life."

"Lorenzo, don't do this man! This is all a big misunderstanding. I swear on my daughter I will have your money tomorrow. Fuck, if you let me leave right now I'll have that shit to you tonight!" I listened to Darnell stutter his words.

My men, who had been patiently waiting in each corner of the warehouse, dressed in all black, loaded with nothing but artillery, stepped out of the darkness ready to obliterate the enemy I had once considered my best worker. Darnell's eyes widened as he witnessed the men who had saved and protected him on numerous occasions, as he dealt with the vultures he encountered in the street life, now ready to end his.

"Don't do this, Zo! Pleeease," Darnell was now on his knees begging.

"Damn, nigga, you already a thief and a backstabber. Don't add, going out crying like a bitch to that too. Man the fuck up. At least take this bullet like a soldier."

“I’m sorry, Zo. Please don’t do this. I gotta daughter that need me. Pleeease man, I’ll do anything. Just don’t kill me.” The tears were pouring down Darnell’s face and instead of softening me up it just made me even more pissed at his punk ass.

“Save your fuckin’ tears. You shoulda thought about your daughter before you stole from me. You’re the worse sort of thief. I invite you into my home, I make you a part of my family and you steal from me, you plot against me. Your daughter doesn’t need you. You have nothing to teach her.”

My men each pulled out their gat ready to attack and I put my hand up motioning them to stop. For the first time since Darnell arrived, a calm gaze spread across his face.

“I knew you didn’t have the heart to let them kill me, Zo. We’ve been through so much together. I mean you Tania’s God Father. We bigger than this and we will get through it,” Darnell said, halfway smiling as he began getting off his knees and standing up.

“You’re right, I don’t have the heart to let them kill you, I’ma do that shit myself.” Darnell didn’t even have a chance to let what I said resonate with him because I just sprayed that muthafucker like the piece of shit he was. “Clean this shit up,” I said, stepping over Darnell’s bullet ridden body as I made my exit.

A KING PRODUCTION

Dior Comes Home...

Rich or Famous Part 2

JOY DEJA KING AND CHRIS BOOKER

A KING PRODUCTION

Love Or Stardom...

Rich or Famous Part 3

JOY DEJA KING

A KING PRODUCTION

MAFIA Princess

The Takeover

PART 5

A NOVEL

JOY DEJA KING

AND CHRIS BOOKER

A KING PRODUCTION

Young Diamond Books

PRESENTS

A young adult urban tale

Ride Wit' Me 2

Order Form

A King Production
P.O. Box 912
Collierville, TN 38027
www.joydejaking.com
www.twitter.com/joydejaking

Name: ______________________________
Address: ______________________________
City/State: ______________________________
Zip: ______________________________

QUANTITY	TITLES	PRICE	TOTAL
____	Bitch	$15.00	______
____	Bitch Reloaded	$15.00	______
____	The Bitch Is Back	$15.00	______
____	Queen Bitch	$15.00	______
____	Last Bitch Standing	$15.00	______
____	Superstar	$15.00	______
____	Ride Wit' Me	$12.00	______
____	Stackin' Paper	$15.00	______
____	Trife Life To Lavish	$15.00	______
____	Trife Life To Lavish II	$15.00	______
____	Stackin' Paper II	$15.00	______
____	Rich or Famous	$15.00	______
____	Rich or Famous Part 2	$15.00	______
____	Bitch A New Beginning	$15.00	______
____	Mafia Princess Part 1	$15.00	______
____	Mafia Princess Part 2	$15.00	______
____	Mafia Princess Part 3	$15.00	______
____	Mafia Princess Part 4	$15.00	______
____	Mafia Princess Part 5	$15.00	______
____	Boss Bitch	$15.00	______
____	Baller Bitches Vol. 1	$15.00	______
____	Baller Bitches Vol. 2	$15.00	______
____	Bad Bitch	$15.00	______
____	Still The Baddest Bitch	$15.00	______
____	Power	$15.00	______
____	Power Part 2	$15.00	______
____	Drake	$15.00	______
____	Drake Part 2	$15.00	______
____	Princess Fever "Birthday Bash"	$9.99	______

Shipping/Handling (Via Priority Mail) $6.50 1-2 Books, $8.95 3-4 Books add $1.95 for ea. Additional book.

Total: $________ FORMS OF ACCEPTED PAYMENTS: Certified or government issued checks and money Orders, all mail in orders take 5-7 Business days to be delivered